With a sof
leaned forw
very gently o

They were close enough for her to feel a
shudder rip though his body, for her ears to
catch the echo of a despairing groan. Then he
touched her lips with his finger—a don't
speak kind of gesture—and took her hand,
holding it tightly in his, his thumb running
over her skin, telling her all kinds of things
his lips could never say.

And right then she knew that tonight would be
their night. A one-off, one and only, but theirs
no matter what.

Dear Reader

Over the last few years I've really enjoyed reading 'relationship' books involving the lives of young, single career women juggling priorities to find enough time for love, friendship, shopping and even basic personal maintenance. Generally, the support network of other single friends keeps them sane, so the idea of helping four friends find love really appealed to me.

Gabi, Kirsten, Alana and Daisy all live in the Near West apartment building, and work or have worked at the Royal Westside Hospital. Gabi, a doctor, has loved and lost. Kirsten, an occupational therapist, has been held in the grip of unrequited love. Nurse Alana's previous venture into romance has left her preferring the company of her pets; though she strongly believes in love, she theorises that it grows from friendship, not attraction. Daisy is a psychologist who can tell them why things happen as they do, but can't quite sort out her own problems.

The four friends share each other's tears and laughter, and, often with unexpected consequences, try to help each other along the rocky road to love.

I have had such fun getting to know these women as I wrote these four books, and I hope you enjoy their company as much as I have.

Meredith Webber

Look out for the last in the WESTSIDE STORIES:

DAISY AND THE DOCTOR (Daisy's story)

Coming soon from Mills & Boon® Medical Romance™

Recent titles by the same author:

DEAR DOCTOR (Kirsten's story)
DR GRAHAM'S MARRIAGE (Gabi's story)

THE DOCTOR'S DESTINY

BY

MEREDITH WEBBER

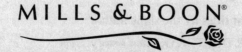

MILLS & BOON®

DID YOU PURCHASE THIS BOOK WITHOUT A COVER?

If you did, you should be aware it is **stolen property** as it was reported *unsold and destroyed* by a retailer. Neither the author nor the publisher has received any payment for this book.

All the characters in this book have no existence outside the imagination of the author, and have no relation whatsoever to anyone bearing the same name or names. They are not even distantly inspired by any individual known or unknown to the author, and all the incidents are pure invention.

All Rights Reserved including the right of reproduction in whole or in part in any form. This edition is published by arrangement with Harlequin Enterprises II B.V. The text of this publication or any part thereof may not be reproduced or transmitted in any form or by any means, electronic or mechanical, including photocopying, recording, storage in an information retrieval system, or otherwise, without the written permission of the publisher.

This book is sold subject to the condition that it shall not, by way of trade or otherwise, be lent, resold, hired out or otherwise circulated without the prior consent of the publisher in any form of binding or cover other than that in which it is published and without a similar condition including this condition being imposed on the subsequent purchaser.

MILLS & BOON and MILLS & BOON with the Rose Device are registered trademarks of the publisher.

First published in Great Britain 2003
Harlequin Mills & Boon Limited,
Eton House, 18-24 Paradise Road, Richmond, Surrey TW9 1SR

© Meredith Webber 2003

ISBN 0 263 83430 1

Set in Times Roman 10½ on 11¼ pt.
03-0303-52684

Printed and bound in Spain
by Litografía Rosés, S.A., Barcelona

CHAPTER ONE

ALANA walked out of the hospital, not with her usual brisk stride but with her feet on autopilot as she pondered the problems she saw developing in her precious Ward Eight B—the admittance ward at Royal Westside Hospital.

'Hey, slowcoach, what's with you?'

She turned towards the source of the voice then wished she'd kept walking.

'Honestly, Kirsten,' she groused at her recently engaged friend. 'You could dim the radiance a little. Happy as I am for you and Josh, this glowing thing you're doing is very depressing for a single, unattached-and-likely-to-remain-that-way thirty-year-old.'

Kirsten simply grinned and glowed a little brighter, making Alana wish she hadn't lost her latest pair of sunglasses.

(Where did all the world's lost sunglasses end up? Sunglass heaven?)

'You're just tired because you've had a long day,' Kirsten said, her overwhelming happiness making allowances for even the grumpiest of friends. 'And why's that, anyway? You've been on seven o'clock starts—seven to three-thirty shifts—so what are you doing walking home at five-thirty?'

Unable to provide an answer—Kirsten might seriously doubt her sanity if she said she'd been up on the ward, staring blankly at her time sheet for the last hour—Alana kept walking.

Not that a little silence would put Kirsten off the scent.

'It's not this hang-up you've got over Rory Forrester again, is it?' she demanded. 'Honestly, Alana, for someone who's never met the new senior physician, you're behaving very strangely.'

'He's disrupting my ward!' Alana stormed, lengthening her stride as anger built. 'Students in an admittance ward! The whole idea's ridiculous. I went along with it for a month at the end of last year, then managed to persuade Ted Ryan, the registrar, that it just wasn't working. The students' year was about to finish anyway, so it wasn't too hard. Now, apparently, the phantom is due back and Ted's got his trousers in a twist over the fact that he hasn't re-instated it. He tells me they start again on Monday week, whether I like it or not!'

'Why are students such a nuisance?' Kirsten asked, as they waited for a break in the traffic before crossing the road. 'I mean, I know there are a lot of them, and they take up time, but why's it worse in Eight B?'

Alana sighed.

'You know they type of patients we get, Kirsten. They're often elderly, they're usually either confused or panicky, and for a lot of them, Eight B's only a brief stopover on their way to somewhere else in the hospital. Depending on what their test results show, they might be transferred to Neurology, or to the renal unit, or slated for surgery and go from Eight B to Theatre then to a surgical recovery area. Most nurses avoid it like the plague, but I love the challenge of helping patients feel comfortable and at ease in the hospital surroundings. It doesn't bother me that they're only temporarily in my care. My job is to see they receive the best possible attention, that they understand at least something of what's happening to them, and what could be happening in the future.'

'And students mess this up?'

'Of course they mess it up!' Alana snorted, when they'd dashed across the road in a small break between two cars and a council truck. 'In order not to be caught out by a question during a round, students straggle in whenever they feel like it and ask patients what's wrong with them, and the whole point of being in Eight B is that no one quite knows what's wrong with them. If renal failure had been picked up down in A and E the patient would have gone straight to the renal ward, ditto acute appendicitis. In Eight B we wait for the results of tests ordered by A and E, and order more if these are inconclusive. The doctors don't know what's wrong with half the patients, so how would the patients?'

Kirsten nodded.

'I can see your point, but as soon as they're through their studies, doing their intern year, most youngsters end up in wards like Eight B doing admittance procedures, so don't they need to see these places?'

Alana glared at her.

'I hate people who argue practicalities,' she muttered. 'And I don't mind them seeing Eight B, even walking through it from time to time, preferably on their way to somewhere else. I just don't want student rounds in *my* ward!'

'Then you'll just have to talk to Rory Forrester about it. I hear he's finally due to start on Monday.' Kirsten paused and looked at her friend. 'Which, no doubt, you've also heard, and which explains why you're so touchy!'

Alana decided the comment didn't deserve a reply. Besides, she could hear the sound of a tennis ball thwacking into the practice wall at the end of the tennis court of the Near West apartment complex.

It reminded her of just how long it had been since she'd had any practice. Winter fixtures began in early April, just over four weeks away.

Deciding a hit-up would be infinitely better than practising alone, she mumbled at Kirsten, 'Ha, a possible tennis partner!' And instead of accompanying her friend up the front steps of the building where they both had flats, she detoured around the side to suggest a game to whoever was on the court.

A skinny kid with the obligatory baseball cap, bill backwards, on his head. He was either visiting someone in the building, or using the court illegally, but as she watched him chase down the balls he spun into the wall, she decided legality didn't matter—he was good.

'Want a game?' she called, startling him into missing a return. *And* into using a swear word she pretended not to hear.

He chased the errant ball, then turned towards her, his arrogant young eyes skimming her far from pristine navy skirt and aqua top and bulky but comfortable work shoes.

'Can you play?'

Arrogant mouth, too!

'A little,' she said, her voice as mild as milk, though she wanted to shake the young brat. 'Give me ten minutes to change?'

He shrugged as if he couldn't care less whether he played with her or not, but Alana knew from experience that playing was far better than hitting practice balls against a wall. He'd play!

She hurried through the back entrance to the foyer, raced up the two flights of stairs, threw off her skirt and top and leapt under the shower, before pulling on an old pair of shorts and a loose T-shirt.

She found a new tube of balls, grabbed her racket and rocketed back down the stairs, intent now not so much on tennis practice but on beating the bratty youngster.

He was practising his serve now, using balls from a bucket he must have brought with him. Serious practice, then, whoever he was.

Alana watched him for a few minutes, admiring his technique, then moved forward to introduce herself.

'I'm Alana Wright. I live on the second floor.'

'Jason McAllister.' His blank-eyed expression told her

that was all the information she was going to get. 'Toss for serve?'

'No, you've been practising, you go right ahead,' Alana told him. 'Best of three? I'll turn on the lights as it will be dark before we finish.'

She offered the tube of balls and he glanced at the label then checked out her racket. She could practically hear his brain assessing her ability at the game, then the smile, matching the eyes in arrogance, told her he'd decided he could beat her anyway—the phrase 'she's only a woman' transmitted as clearly as if he'd spoken it.

Jason *was* good. And he was younger and faster, and had obviously not missed as much practice as she had over the summer, but he hadn't had an extremely frustrating day in Ward Eight B and didn't have a whole lot of anger to work off.

He won the first set easily, but she took the second in a tie-break and, using every ounce of guile she'd developed over the years, broke his first service game in the third set and hung on grimly to win two sets to one.

'Best of five?' he suggested, which was as close to conceding defeat as his youth would allow.

Alana grinned at him.

'You've got to be kidding. I haven't been practising, and after this little effort I probably won't be able to walk tomorrow.'

'Most people let kids win!' he grumbled, almost but not quite under his breath.

'I'm not most people and it doesn't do your tennis any good to have people letting you win,' Alana countered. 'But you're not bad and we made a game of it. Do you live around here? Would you like to play a regular game with me? Or even occasionally?'

The blank-eyed stare returned, and the lad shrugged then began to collect some stray practice balls from over by the fence.

Alana waited, but he obviously wasn't going to reply so in the end she said, 'Well, thanks for the game. I'm in Unit 2A on the second floor of this building, if ever you want someone to knock up with. I'm usually home from work by four-thirty and until fixtures start I'm available most afternoons.'

He didn't answer, simply picking up his bucket of balls and walking towards the gate. When he'd opened it, he paused, turned back towards her and nodded, and she could have sworn she heard a whispered, 'Thanks.' But it was the look in his eyes that remained with her—a look that encompassed loss and despair and such empty nothingness it was like being sucked into a deep black hole.

She switched off the lights and left the courts, wondering, as the lock on the gate snicked shut, how Jason had found his way in. All the tenants had keys, but Near West apartment building was home to mainly young—OK, youngish—mostly medical people who worked at the nearby Royal Westside hospital. The Frosts, in the penthouse, had infant twin boys, but as nominal landlords of the building, by virtue of the fact Madeleine Frost's father owned it, they rarely leased to other families, preferring singles or perhaps newly married couples.

No one she knew in the building owned a teenager.

She made her way back to her unit and was unlocking her door when Daisy Rutherford, a psychologist who had the other unit on the second floor, emerged from the opposite door.

'Off to work?' Alana asked, and Daisy nodded, but this evening her smile didn't seem quite as serene.

'Getting sick of your vampirish working hours?' Alana teased, and Daisy grimaced.

'I don't think it's the night work that's getting me down, although the hours I work mean I don't get to have a proper life.' She released a breath that in anyone else might have been taken for a sigh, but Daisy was so together it couldn't possibly have been one. 'It's the people who contact me. I mean, I have parents phone in for advice about their toddlers or teenagers, I give it to them, and do they take any notice? Not a bit. They ring again the next night and ask the same questions. That was one of the reasons I changed the focus of the show to include a segment for kids to phone in themselves, but I think that was a mistake. I've got ten-year-olds phoning up at ten o'clock at night to tell me their parents keep making them go to bed, and twelve-year-olds complaining because their mothers think they're too young for sex.'

Alana chuckled.

'I thought that's what psychology was all about, providing an outlet for people who need to get things off their chests.'

'You can do that at the complaints department of the local department store,' Daisy growled at her, then she pressed the button to summon the lift, and found a reasonable facsimile of her usual smile. 'Or in the foyer of your building if you're lucky enough to live near Alana,' she added. She smiled as she stepped into the lift, and added her punchline, 'I'm thinking of giving it up and going back to real people rather than voices on a phone!'

Alana walked into her flat, shaking her head over this revelation of another side of Daisy, who was usually the most placid, sunny-tempered and quietly optimistic of women. And who, up till now, had always seemed to love her job.

Maybe her own mood was being reflected in other people, Alana decided, as the cat wound its way around her legs, reminding her it was way past feeding time.

'OK,' she told it. 'I'll see to you now.'

But before she'd finished washing out his water bowl, the phone rang.

Alana studied the instrument for a moment then decided there was absolutely no one in the entire world with whom she wished to speak, so she let the answering machine, still turned on, pick it up.

Kirsten's voice.

'Come on, Alana, we know you're there. We've just seen Daisy. Get out of your tennis gear and come down to Mickey's for a drink. Gabi and Alex are here, but Josh is working so you can keep me company.'

'No, thanks,' Alana said, picking up the receiver as ordered and hoping she sounded firm rather than bloody-minded. 'I haven't fed the animals, and when that's done, I've got "me" stuff to do. Hair-washing, leg-shaving, and general depilatory and maintenance processes. You know the kind of thing.'

Kirsten protested she could do all that the following day—what else were weekends for?

'Shopping, for one thing,' Alana told her. 'The only human edibles in the flat are a rind of cheese, a slice of bread and a tin of artichoke hearts. If I don't do a major shop tomorrow, I'll be fighting Biddy for her guinea-pig food and, believe me, I wouldn't want to win.'

Kirsten argued lack of food was a good reason to eat at Mickey's, the bistro connected to the bar on the ground floor, but Alana remained firm.

'Tonight's an at-home night,' she said, then she said goodbye and hung up, leaving the answering machine on to handle any further invitations.

Not that there was likely to be a rush of them.

She went about her tasks with no regrets, finally settling into a foaming bubble bath with a book, a glass of white wine and every intention of relaxing there for some time to come.

But the wine failed to relax her and the bath failed to soothe, the frustrations of the day refusing to be washed away by sudsy water.

Was it the job itself? Had she become too involved with

Ward Eight B? Was this involvement making her exagger-
ate the student problem?

She sighed and sank beneath the water, feeling her long
hair mingling with the bubbles. She'd wash it under the
shower when she'd finished, she decided, then, as the problem seemed no easier to solve underwater than it had been
above it, she sat up again, pushing soap and hair off her
face, wondering if it was time for a career move.

This question was still fluttering in Alana's head some
twenty hours later as she dressed for the first night of a
concert she'd particularly wanted to attend—back in
September when she'd read the full programme for the
summer concert season. Tonight, however, Mahler's
Symphony No. 1 and a cello concerto by a composer she
didn't know lacked the appeal they had held for her last
spring, and only the fact that she'd just happened to catch
sight of a divine designer trouser suit as she'd shopped, and
it had just happened to fit, so she'd just happened to buy
it, so she now really needed to wear it out to justify the
expense, was forcing her along to the State Theatre.

Reluctance made her late, so the lights were already
dimmed and the orchestra tuning up as she made her way
to her seat, murmuring hellos and apologies to the regulars
in the seats between the aisle and her allotted position.

She managed to get as far as the seat next to hers before
she finally trod on someone's toe—Mrs Schnitzerling's toe,
in fact. Mrs had shifted Mr to the other side of their pair
of seats very early on in the season.

Apologising quietly, Alana sank down into her own padded chair, grateful for the darkness that had covered her
floundering arrival. She reached out automatically to dump
her handbag on the seat next to hers—a seat that had been
vacant for the entire season.

But not tonight.

Her handbag struck a solid block she assumed was a

body. A large-sized body, which a quick embarrassed glance proved to be male. Panic skittered through her, though why she'd be panicking over someone finally taking that seat she had no idea.

Perhaps it was embarrassment, not panic.

She murmured another apology, then, because she didn't want creases in the new suit, leant forward to tuck her handbag under her seat instead. But she missed the space somehow and in the confusion managed to grab the man's leg, which led to the third apology in as many minutes.

And more panic and/or embarrassment.

The arrival of the conductor and the loud applause which greeted him should have settled things down, but though she tried to relax and let the music do its work, freeing her from the everyday world, her muscles refused to oblige, remaining tense—all her nerves standing to attention, as if aware of some imminent danger.

Refusing to believe it could have anything to do with the man in the seat beside her, she nonetheless decided she needed to get a better look at him. Not easy to do while keeping her head turned towards the stage so he didn't know she was looking.

Squinting sideways didn't help much, though her olfactory senses picked up on a faint hint of masculine aftershave—an undertone of citrus blended with something fresh like gum leaves—while her other senses offered a general impression of height and solidity.

Male solidity.

Very male solidity.

She grinned to herself in the darkness.

Because the seat had been empty since the beginning of the season, she and her friends had joked about the possibility of the man of her dreams turning up in it one night.

Not that she had a dream man—not one defined by height or looks or colouring, or even profession or nature. If asked to clarify this vagueness, she'd explain that she was sure she'd know if he did turn up, because he'd be a friend first and friendship would develop into love. Then, to stop the nonsense the others might indulge in, she'd add, firmly, that in the meantime she was happy with her life as it was.

Except that she wasn't, was she?

But surely that was to do with work?

Loud applause from the audience reminded her she was here to listen to music, not worry about perfect men— should such animals exist—or her job. The prelude was over, and the concert was under way.

As the music swelled and ran with a variation, finally lifting her out of herself into the rarefied air of the senses, she felt the tension slide out of her nerves and her body relax.

But not slump! She mustn't slump into Mrs S., who could sleep through half a concert without slumping, or against the man in the spare seat. Slumping on him would be worse than hitting him with her handbag and grabbing at his leg.

She squinted his way again, this time turning her head far enough to see the straight, strong profile of a man not young but certainly not old.

Distracting, though—possibly because she'd become used to the spare seat.

Definitely not because he was a man, and as such was exuding masculine vibrations into the air around him—her air in fact.

But as the music soared, violins chasing the flutes up the scale, lifting and lifting until all the instruments joined in a wildly enthusiastic repetition of the theme, crashing to a whisper before rising again to a triumphant conclusion, her awareness of the man failed to diminish. In fact, it expanded, as if in tandem with the symphony, so, far from slumping, Alana felt her body growing more and more rigid.

Because of a man's presence by her side?

Impossible!

Because a straight, almost severe profile had affected her?

Doubly impossible.

She sneaked another look as the audience applauded then, shamed and confused by the way her mind was working—it had to be due to the fact she and her friends had joked about the seat—she turned away from him, leaning towards Mr and Mrs Schnitzerling, to ask, as she always did, if they'd enjoyed the first part of the concert.

By the time the couple had given their opinions of the visiting conductor—excellent but flashy—the guest first violin—knows her stuff—and the programme in general—better than last month—most of the audience had departed, including the newcomer who'd been sitting on the other side of Alana.

He must have headed for the far aisle rather than interrupt by walking past them.

She felt a twinge of regret that she hadn't seen him in the light, but there'd be another chance later, when he returned to his seat.

Muscles which had relaxed—slightly—during her conversation with her concert neighbours tensed again at the thought.

Maybe if she saw him in the light—went out to the foyer and had a good look—she'd be able to settle down. But would she find him? Surely there couldn't be all that many tall, solid men with straight strong profiles at the concert tonight...

'Aren't you coming out to stretch your legs?' Mrs Schnitzerling asked, and Alana shook her head.

Searching the foyer for a man?

She must be out of her mind!

She'd stay right where she was, breathe deeply and get

over whatever it was that had affected her during the first session.

Besides, if she remained in her seat, she'd get a good view of him when he returned. Seeing him as a person, not just a profile, should cure whatever ailed her. He probably had deep frown lines, betraying a fearsome temper, and wore a wedding ring, keeping him off-limits even if he didn't have a fearsome temper.

Just thinking such thoughts made her sigh.

It had to be the problems she was having—or anticipating having—at work which had her so uptight and had her entertaining such ridiculous thoughts.

But she *would* look at him when he returned to his seat. After all, she could hardly avoid it.

If he'd returned to his seat!

'You're sure you'd remembered deodorant?' Kirsten asked, when she, Daisy and Alana had met for breakfast at a local coffee-shop next morning and Alana was explaining the mystery man's appearance then disappearance.

'Deodorant *and* a little designer perfume,' Alana replied. 'Though maybe that was it. Maybe he was allergic to perfume. People are, you know.'

'Then they shouldn't go to concerts where other people are sure to be wearing it,' Kirsten retorted, while Alana remembered a certain aftershave and decided it couldn't have been an allergy to her perfume that had caused the disappearance of her fellow concert-lover.

'I don't think it *was* the aftershave,' she muttered to herself—or not quite to herself if the others' reaction was any guide.

'What wasn't the aftershave?' Kirsten demanded, while Daisy merely echoed the final word.

'The—I suppose awareness is the word I'm after, but it's not strong enough to explain how conscious I was of him.

It was weird. Still is, because I can close my eyes and see his profile, and feel whatever it was I felt then.'

She turned to Daisy with an embarrassed grin.

'Please, assure me I'm not going mad—or entering some disastrous phase of a woman's life where she's turned on by profiles.'

Daisy offered her usual calming smile.

'You know, if the aftershave wasn't strong, it could be that the man's natural scent came through. I was reading an article where, in a properly constituted scientific study, a group of men were asked to wear the same T-shirt for four days. These were then put into plastic bags, and women were asked to choose a man on the basis of the smell.'

'Oh, gross!' Kirsten cried, holding her hand across her nose at the thought. 'Though I guess socks would be worse.'

They all laughed but the idea intrigued Alana, who was desperate for a rational explanation for her reaction, so when things settled down again, she asked, 'And what did this prove? Did the winner of the smelly T-shirt competition get the girl? It doesn't sound very scientific to me.'

Daisy chuckled.

'It was, and all the women chose a different man, then when the men and women were tested, it showed that in every case the women, based solely on smell, had chosen the man with the immunity system most different to theirs. The researchers argued that this made mate selection more effective as the couples would have the widest possible range of genetic difference to pass on to their children.'

'I bet he was wearing a suit,' Kirsten said, and Alana, who was still thinking about mate selection, raised her eyebrows at her friend.

'Well,' Kirsten explained, 'men wear suits more than once between dry-cleaning, so maybe their natural scent gets caught in the fibres and enough of that remains to overcome things like aftershave.'

'Given they also wear shirts and underwear next to their bodies, it's more likely to be dry-cleaning fluid caught in the fibres.' Alana squashed this theory, then she sighed. 'So I'm attracted to men who smell like dry-cleaning fluid. Great!'

The others laughed but her concern remained. Not long ago, Kirsten had admitted to feeling something Alana had heartlessly put down to 'nesting syndrome'. Surely she wasn't suffering the same thing!

And why?

Because a stranger had sat beside her at the concert?

Maybe it was time she agreed to meet Jeremy, the man she'd first spoken to in an internet chat room, and with whom, from the frequent emails they'd exchanged, she seemed to have a lot in common. Maybe a normal relationship would put a stop to whatever subconscious stuff was going on.

Yet the scent of the aftershave seemed to have lodged in her senses so she could smell it now, and she was recalling the autocratic profile to her visual memory when she realised Kirsten was speaking again. Something about a problem in the building. Fire brigade?

'Why was the fire brigade called?' she asked, needing clarification before she could follow the story.

'Because of the cat. I thought it was your cat—not Stubby but the stray you feed—but apparently it belonged to the new people on the third floor, in the unit under Gabi's, and when it got out the boy tried to get it off the ledge between the balconies and he got stuck. Hence the fire brigade who brought ladders.'

'Did they get the cat? Was the cat all right?' Alana asked, and Daisy laughed.

'We might have known you'd be more interested in the

cat. It was fine. It came down long before the fire engines arrived.'

Daisy seemed about to say something more when Kirsten spoke again, telling them about a cat who'd adopted Mrs Phillips, her fiancé's mother, which hissed and spat whenever a man came near it.

'But what I want to know,' Kirsten finished, 'is how the cat knows the difference between human sexes. I mean, I can go out there in jeans and a T-shirt and it rubs against my legs. Josh appears in identical clothing, and the hissing stuff begins.'

'We're back on the scents we humans give off,' Daisy suggested. 'I imagine a sense of smell is far more highly developed in animals and that's how the cat tells.'

Alana nodded her agreement, adding, 'Yes, intelligent as cats are, I doubt they realise one human sex generally has long hair and the other short. A lot of the time these days even I can't tell at first glance. So it has to be some other sense.'

The conversation lingered in Alana's mind when she returned home, and she found herself wondering if it had only been the aftershave that had made her so certain—right from the start—that the person next to her at the concert was a man. Or had she subconsciously picked up a masculine scent?

A masculine scent that was attractive to her immune system?

No way! The only time she ever gave her immune system even a passing thought was on the rare occasions she picked up a cold—and then she'd give it a talking to for letting her down.

'At least I didn't hiss or spit!' she joked to herself, as she put food out on the balcony for the stray who hadn't caused the problem the previous night. Thinking of that story—anything was better than thinking about 'the man'—she peered upwards, wondering who'd shifted in above her.

The flat had been vacant for ages, leased, though not inhabited for some reason neither of the Frosts had been willing to share.

Had the boy involved in the previous night's drama been her tennis partner?

Was that where he'd come from?

The flats on her side of the building were all two-bedroomed, which would allow enough room for a couple and one child, two children if they were small and shared. On the other side were single-bedroom dwellings, the space for the stairwell and lift taken from where the second bedroom would have been.

But children?

Was Near West changing its image? Going for family tenants now?

Would she eventually have to leave her home as well as her job?

She shook away the stupid train of thought. There was no reason on earth why she should leave Near West.

She stared out over the roofs of neighbouring houses, looking towards the hospital.

Or leave her job!

A sudden clatter from the balcony above made her move back towards the sliding glass doors, then a slim, elegant Siamese sprang down onto her balcony railing, studied her with incurious blue eyes for a moment, then leapt again—either to its death or to the balcony below.

'Damn you!' someone yelled, then legs appeared, feet feeling for the same railing, finding it, steadying, then dropping lightly onto the floor in front of her.

'Couldn't find the door, Jason?' she said, and saw his start of surprise when he realised she was standing watching him.

'It's the cat!' he told her, anger emanating from him like heat waves from the bitumen on a hot day. 'The vet said to keep her inside for three days, but the moment I open the door she's out.'

He looked anxiously around, so obviously worried that Alana felt a reluctant sympathy for him.

'Cats can make their way back to their old homes across thousands of miles,' he added, voicing the fear and uncertainty she could see in his eyes. 'I saw a movie about it once. A true movie. I don't want it to do that.'

'Maybe she's just checking out her new territory. Being shut in might make her feel there's something out there she's missing, and she wants to look around. How long have you been here?'

'Three days,' he mumbled, turning his back to her to peer down into the garden. 'But I let her out last night too, and the Dungeon Master didn't half go off his block.'

'The Dungeon Master?' Alana echoed, but Jason wasn't listening. He was whistling softly to the cat which had appeared on the path that encircled the building.

'She's just there,' he said, ignoring her query. 'Do you mind if I go through your place to the lift so I can get her?'

'I'd far rather you did that than tried the balcony trick again,' Alana said. 'Think of the blood on the path if you missed your footing. But before you go, I'll give you some cookies which cats just love. Darren, at the local pet shop, makes them to a secret recipe.'

She led the way into her flat but, though Jason followed, he didn't come far, stopped first by the sight of her featherless parrot, then further distracted by the guinea-pig cage, fish tank and large box that currently housed an injured rabbit.

'Look at all these pets. How come you're allowed to have them in a flat? I thought I was lucky being allowed to keep my cat. But I guess that was the Dungeon Master's decree, not the flat owner's.'

He was offering his finger to the guinea pigs, trying to coax the babies out of their box.

'It was my mother's cat,' he added, almost in an undertone, and once again Alana was struck by a vulnerability beneath the cocky veneer of the young teenager. 'I suppose that's why he let me keep it.'

Was 'he' the man Jason had called the Dungeon Master? His father?

And did the unflattering nickname mean he kept the kid on a tight rein?

'Why don't you get your cat then come back to check out the animals?' Alana suggested. 'She can meet my cat, Stubby.'

At the sound of his name, Stubby emerged from under a chair, blinked sleepily at Alana, then leapt lightly up onto the chair, apparently so he could get into better sniffing distance of Jason.

More olfactory senses getting a workout!

'No tail—is that why he's called Stubby?' Jason stroked the broad, butting head. 'Is he a Manx cat?'

'No, just a fighter! Or he was. That's how he lost his tail. He had it torn in a fight and infection set in. The vet had to remove it. Then his owners thought he looked so odd he should be put down, which is how I got to have him.'

Jason shook his head, gave Stubby one last pat, then, taking the small biscuit Alana offered, he left the flat.

Alana moved back onto the balcony, hoping to spot the Siamese for him. Not hard, when it was sitting grooming itself in the sun, immediately below her balcony.

Jason appeared and approached with caution then held out the biscuit. The cat yawned to show she really wasn't interested, then stood up and picked her way delicately towards him, condescending to nibble on the biscuit but refusing to show any affection or closeness.

'Cats!' Jason said, grinning up at her. Then his grin faded and as a mutinous expression took its place, she wondered what she'd done to upset him. Until she realised he was looking beyond her—higher.

'The DM,' he mouthed at her, scooping up the cat and disappearing from view.

Moments later, he knocked on her front door.

'I've got to go, but thanks for the biscuit, and if it's OK with you, I'd like to come back and look at your animals some other time.'

He was gone before she had time to answer, making for the stairs rather than the lift, pausing, as he opened the fire door, to throw a cheeky smile over his shoulder.

'I make up names for people. Want to know yours?'

Not particularly, Alana thought, but, remembering the vulnerability she'd sensed earlier, she nodded anyway.

'Dragon Lady!' he said, then he disappeared into the stairwell, the heavy fire-door shutting slowly and noiselessly behind him.

Alana smiled to herself. Would he have called her something nicer if she'd let him win the tennis game?

CHAPTER TWO

ALANA was up at sunrise the next morning, feeding her animals, setting out fresh water for them, then moping around the flat because it was far too early to go to work.

In the end, she set off anyway, knowing there'd have been a number of new admissions over the weekend and determined to be on top of who was who in case the elusive Rory Forrester finally arrived.

He'd been appointed as senior physician in the internal medicine department months ago, and had apparently spent at least a week in the hospital. And though Alana hadn't met him, she'd felt the wind from the new broom he'd wielded.

Then just as suddenly, he'd gone. Personal problems, someone had said, while had others suggested it had been illness, or a better offer from a hospital overseas.

Now he was back, and for some unknown reason determined to get involved with Eight B—a ward generally ignored by the senior physicians. Consultant specialists dropped in—it was another of Alana's bugbears that they never came on time—to see patients who might eventually come under their care, but the senior physicians in the past had been content to let Eight B run itself.

Maybe he'd get over it. Maybe he'd come once then never come again. Maybe he'd listen to reason if she spoke to him about the students.

Maybe the moon would turn blue!

Reaching the hospital, she shut the possible problems away in the far reaches of her mind, though it was already crowded back there with the smelly T-shirt syndrome and the profile.

Forget the profile, think of work. She would *not* let things that might not happen bother her.

Half an hour before change of shift, the corridors were quiet, the foyers empty of people. Enjoying the sensation of being alone in a place where she knew there were over a thousand inhabitants, she smiled to herself, and was still smiling when the lift doors opened and she stepped inside.

Rory Forrester, wedged behind one of the complicated cleaning trolleys the housekeeping staff trundled endlessly along hospital corridors, glimpsed the smile first.

Or perhaps he noticed it because it was Monday morning, and he was by nature a Monday-morning grump. This particular Monday morning he'd had so many added pressures, work had seemed like the best option.

So the smile irritated him, and the fact that it had widened, and brightened—sparkled, in fact—when she greeted the porter with the trolley was an added annoyance.

He studied the smilee—or what he could see of her past the mop and broom heads behind which he stood—as, apparently oblivious of anyone else in the lift, she chatted with the middle-aged man. A tall, slim, fit-looking woman, with shiny blonde hair pulled back into a neat knot at the back of her head. Her skin was lightly tanned, and there was an air of freshness and enthusiasm about her that was all out of kilter with what he thought of as 'hospital Mondayitis'.

She seemed vaguely familiar, not as someone he'd met in his brief preliminary sojourn at Royal Westside but maybe someone he'd seen on a ward.

She was also, not at all vaguely, attractive. Conventionally so in a neat controlled way, but also in the sense that he felt the elusive tug of the physical magnetism—that kind of attraction—which drew men to women.

Hoots of mocking laughter sounded in his head. With a backlog of five months' work to catch up on, and seemingly insurmountable personal problems to sort out, he'd have no time for even the smallest dalliance—should he be so foolish as to even contemplate such a thing.

But his physical self must be feeling the effects of what was beginning to seem like permanent celibacy, because it was the second time he'd felt that tug of attraction recently.

The first had been as recently as Saturday night.

Another place, and another blonde—that one in a severe black suit, which had contrasted sharply, and incredibly sexily, with the long blonde hair cascading across her shoulders. He'd tried to ignore her but had then decided it was fate, and had intended introducing himself during the interval, but his pager had vibrated against his hip during the last movement and he'd had to leave the concert as soon as he'd decently been able to.

Rory closed his eyes at the memory of Saturday night's drama, sighed deeply and rubbed his hand through his overlong hair. He'd better learn to live with frustration, because he suspected celibacy was going to become a way of life for a long time into the future.

The lift stopped and the woman got out, followed by the man with the cart. Rory glanced at the floor indicator lights and cursed softly. Surely he'd pressed four, where his office was located. Had the thing stopped and he'd not noticed—too busy brooding over his problems? Or a slim, tanned blonde?

Though while he was on the eighth floor he could check out the admissions ward, Eight B, which came under his overall control. Unfortunately, just as he made this decision—which had nothing to do with the blonde—the lift doors closed, and he was whisked back down to the basement car park where he started all over again.

Alana ignored the comments about her early arrival, settling herself on a spare chair at the nurses' station and tapping the computer keyboard to get rid of the screen saver and bring up some patient details. She smiled to herself—she wasn't the only one fretting about the new specialist's arrival. Rex Jones, the cleaner on Eight, had come on duty early to make sure the new man, should he visit the wards on his first day, could find no fault with the floors.

'I know Mrs Armstrong, don't I?' she said to no one in particular when the first new patient's name flashed across the screen. As no one answered, she read the notes and realised she did know the woman, who'd been admitted with severe anaemia towards the end of the previous year. Endoscopy, where a tube with a miniature camera on it was inserted down her throat and into her stomach, had revealed bleeding polyps in her stomach, and although these had been cauterised on her last admission, it was now possible more had ruptured.

Leaving the computer, Alana walked through to see the elderly woman.

'I'm so glad you're still here,' Mrs Armstrong greeted her. 'Apart from Sue, who was on duty last night, everyone else is new.'

Alana perched on the side of the bed, automatically registering the woman's rosy colour, no doubt as a result of the blood transfusion she'd been given the previous evening, and bandages down one side of her head.

'What happened this time?' Alana asked.

Mrs Armstrong looked embarrassed.

'So silly. I must have fainted, and I hit my head. Fortunately Alf got hungry and when I wouldn't feed him—I was lying on the floor, out cold—he went over to my neighbour's because she fed him when I was in hospital last time, and he thought he might scrounge a meal over there.'

Mrs Armstrong smiled.

'At least, that's what I think. My neighbour, she says Alf went over to tell her I needed help, but cats wouldn't do that, would they?'

Alana was pleased Mrs Armstrong had mentioned cats—she'd been thinking Alf must have been a relative and won-

dering why he'd gone next door for food rather than phoning an ambulance himself.

'Anyway, Jenny, that's my neighbour, phoned the ambulance, and here I am. I have to see someone about my
polyps again, because if it's not them making me weak and
stupid, it might be something else.'

Alana lifted Mrs Armstrong's file, wondering if other
tests had already been carried out or suggested, but there
was no indication of what might be going on. The admitting
doctor in A and E had ordered the blood transfusion when
the first blood tests had showed up the severity of the anaemia, but that was as far as the investigation had progressed.

'I want to go home!'

The querulous voice echoed around the eight-bed room.

'That woman always wants to go home,' Mrs Armstrong
said, nodding towards the gaunt, dishevelled woman in the
bed opposite her. 'She's been saying it all night. But it's
obvious she can't because she'd never be able to look after
herself.'

She tapped her head significantly, and said, 'I might be
passing out at times, but at least my brain's still working.'

Alana nodded.

Bessie Oliver had been in Eight B for nearly a week now,
Ted Ryan conspiring with the nursing staff to keep her as
long as possible while the social work department tried desperately to find her a placement in a nursing home.

Excusing herself from Mrs Armstrong, Alana crossed to
Bessie, knowing the confused woman often quietened if
someone sat with her for a while.

'Hello, Bessie. I'm Alana. I'm one of your nurses. I hope
you enjoyed your breakfast. Cereal and eggs, that's what
you usually have, isn't it?'

Rheumy brown eyes met hers, and although Bessie
didn't answer, she seemed more at ease.

Alana straightened her bed linen, talking all the time,
hoping her voice might soothe the patient enough that she'd

doze off. A hope dashed when a voice, not loud but certainly carrying, penetrated the air.

'Good morning, ladies. No, I'm wrong. We've got one gent. Good morning, ladies and gentleman. I'm Rory Forrester and although you haven't met me before, I'm actually your doctor.'

As soon as he'd given the general introduction, Rory felt stupid, but when the nurse at the desk—Sue something—had led him into the big room, the first person he'd seen had been the blonde from the lift.

She was still smiling—this time at an addled-looking woman in a bed on the far side of the room—and once again the smile—this early on a Monday morning—had thrown him so much he'd behaved like a circus ringmaster entering his domain.

He scowled at the blonde.

It was the fact she looked so healthy—like a sleek, fit animal—that made her so attractive, he decided as Sue led him forward to meet the first patient. She probably jogged, he added gloomily to himself, as moving reminded him of the aches and pains in his back and leg from his recent foray into exercise—a race up three flights of stairs which he'd lost to his thirteen-year-old opponent.

Lost? He'd been tempted to call in paramedics to revive him!

Alana stared at the man. Tall and rangy, he had soft wavy black hair, badly in need of a trim, flopping down over a high forehead and curling slightly just above his ears. His skin was pale, suggesting his eyes might be blue, but it was too far away to see their colour. She felt a shiver of apprehension, and told herself it was because the man had been upsetting her life even before she'd met him, though her body was registering a strange sensation of familiarity.

Which definitely couldn't have anything to do with how he smelt, because he wasn't within smelling distance.

He was introducing himself to each patient in turn and she took the opportunity to look more closely at him.

Of course she'd never met him. He was undoubtedly a 'once seen never forgotten' kind of man.

Yet…

Work! Alana reminded herself, though trying to inject a stern note into mental orders was difficult.

As the Eight B charge nurse and senior nurse on the day shift, she should have been at the desk to meet him. Though Sue Croft was still here and they hadn't done the handover so Sue was nominally in charge. Anyway, Sue was enjoying the moment—leading the specialist forward, introducing him to each patient, talking and waving her hands and looking admiringly up into his eyes.

For a moment, Alana wished she could make the vomiting noise Kirsten did so well, then, surprised by the strength of her reaction, considered whether she *might just* be feeling a faint twinge of what *might just* have been envy.

Oh, please! Get with it here!

Mentally berating herself for entertaining such stupid thoughts, she spoke again to Bessie, though a stray flash of resentment that Sue would have had the opportunity to check his eye colour did intrude momentarily.

The pair reached Bessie's bed, where Alana had remained, mainly because she wasn't certain what else to do.

'This is Alana Wright, Eight B's charge nurse. She should have been the one meeting you this morning, but you were early and Alana hadn't done the handover with me so she couldn't have given you the latest information. Alana, this is Dr Forrester.'

Alana's polite greeting dead-heated with an appraising kind of 'Ah!' from the specialist, and she realised Ted had probably told him about her student ban. And possibly a few other of the gripes Alana generally had about the medical staff's behaviour on Ward Eight B.

Blue. The eyes were blue, with flecks and a rim of darker

blue, so she guessed in some lights they'd look almost black.

Sue was still speaking but, having developed a habit of tuning out about three-quarters of what Sue said, Alana barely heard. Too busy studying Rory Forrester as he spoke quietly to Bessie—too busy trying to work out why he seemed familiar.

At least he was talking to Bessie before he picked up her file. Too many of the doctors, including the specialists, tended to put the file notes first, studying them while they might or might not speak to the patient. Eyes on the notes, not on the person they were treating. As if notes could tell more than people!

She gave him a small tick, but it didn't balance the very large cross against his name on account of the students.

'I'll be starting student rounds next week,' he said, the timing so spot on she could have sworn he'd stolen the word out of her thoughts. But he was still flipping through pages on Bessie's file, so she guessed he couldn't be checking out the inside of her head at the same time.

'I'd like to talk to you about that,' she replied. 'Preferably before they start.'

He glanced at his watch.

'I've a meeting with Admin shortly, but I'll try to get back here later in the day. In the meantime, can you tell me why Mrs Oliver is here?'

Alana hesitated and Sue Croft leapt into the breach.

'Kind-hearted staff,' she responded. 'But, of course, they're day shift staff making the decisions. It's easier for the day shift when more nurses are on duty to help, so they don't bear the brunt of her irrational behaviour.'

A dark eyebrow cocked in Alana's direction.

'She was admitted with a badly ulcerated leg, which is still healing. It's hard to give Bessie IV antibiotics as she pulls out the tube, so she's been having them orally and we've been treating the wound as well.'

For a moment she thought she might get away with this bland but carefully edited explanation, but the eyebrow remained cocked and the look on the man's face told her he'd wait until she offered more.

'She lives with her granddaughter who usually manages her just fine, but Bessie's general health is deteriorating, and the senility is increasing, and at the moment Prue, the granddaughter, is newly pregnant and sick with it. She has a two-year-old and a four-year-old, and just can't cope at present. The ulcer developing to the stage it did was an indication of that, because normally Prue is an excellent carer.'

She looked Rory Forrester in the eyes, and dared him to argue, but surprisingly enough he nodded.

'No respite beds available?'

'Not for dementia sufferers. Not at the moment. What Bessie really needs is a permanent placement in a nursing home because, with three small children, Prue just won't be able to manage her, no matter how much she might want to.'

'Well, as long as we don't need the bed,' the specialist said, and Alana was compelled to give him another small tick.

But two ticks didn't balance out the cross either.

He walked away, accompanied by Sue, though he did turn to nod to Alana before he left the room and paused by the nurses' station to shake hands with Sue, before heading out of the ward.

'My, but he's a handsome one, isn't he?' Mrs Armstrong said, and one of the other women agreed, going on to tell her fellow patients how he looked just like her nephew Phil.

Maybe that's why he'd seemed familiar, Alana decided. He looked like someone else she knew.

But he didn't. Well, no one she could think of, and surely she'd remember someone so darkly good-looking, so dangerously and elementally attractive that she was reminded of a panther or some other big, untamable cat.

'Cats seem to be a theme lately,' she muttered to herself as, ashamed of her fantasies, she made her way out of the room to listen to Sue's account of the night's activities.

A woman who'd been admitted at midnight with the pain usually associated with kidney stones was due to be transferred to the renal unit when a bed became available later in the day. The sole man in the big room where Mrs Armstrong was had been admitted the previous day with severe chest pains, and when the ECG carried out in A and E hadn't revealed any anomalies, further tests had been ordered, which explained why he was with them rather than down in Coronary Care.

The other patients were the usual mix of elderly people being stabilised in some way—dehydration being a major problem with the hot weather still hanging around—and younger people undergoing tests as various doctors tried to determine what was wrong with them.

These younger patients were in single or two-bed rooms ranged along the other side of the nurses' station, while, next to the eight-bed room, a smaller four-bed room was given over to elderly patients whose main problems were caused by the general deterioration of age. Mr Briggs, who had end-stage emphysema, lifted a hand in greeting when Alana walked in, but even that small effort caused an increase in the wheezing, gasping effort as he dragged oxygen through the nasal tube into his diseased lungs.

Mrs Briggs, as ever, sat by his side, and though the staff assured Alana the old woman went home at night, she was always there first thing in the morning. Just sitting quietly beside her husband, talking occasionally, but more often simply letting her presence calm the dying man.

'It's such a strain on her,' Alana said later, talking to Will James, the nurse in charge of the four-bed room this shift.

'Just goes to show you should never do your kids a favour,' Will said, then he ducked his head and edged away.

'Never do your kids a favour?' a deep voice repeated, and Alana swung around to see Rory Forrester standing behind her.

'Mr and Mrs Briggs. Mr Briggs is in bed sixteen,' she said, thankful her voice wasn't behaving as badly as her legs, which were shaking so much she doubted she'd be able to stand. The man had no right to creep up on her and startle her like that! 'They agreed to let their son and his family move into their house, keeping only one big room for themselves. Now Mr Briggs is dying, there's really nothing we can do for him that a visiting nurse couldn't do at home, but the daughter-in-law wants the big room, eventually, for her younger daughter and she doesn't want Mr Briggs dying in it first. She claims the girl, who's all of three, would remember and not feel right in it.'

The specialist frowned and shook his head, and Alana regretted her little outburst. Obviously this man felt the same way as the daughter-in-law—or at least felt nursing staff shouldn't be involving themselves in matters beyond their work.

No doubt he was one of those medical people forever repeating the adage, 'Don't get too involved with your patients, as it can impact on your efficiency.'

Though it *was* her work—that was the whole point. A lot of patients came into Eight B because of lack of care—or caring—in their home situations, and treating them simply for whatever condition they were presenting at the time wasn't good enough as far as Alana was concerned. Many of these people had to have support systems set up for them before they were discharged, while others, without family to speak for them, needed an advocate to make sure they received the very best of care.

But the specialist was talking, and she should be listening. She caught the word 'students' and remembered why he'd come back.

'I don't mind students doing rounds with you, or Ted, or any of the consultants who visit the ward. What I do object to is students wandering in and out at all hours and asking patients questions most of them can't answer.'

'Because they're like Bessie?'

The blue eyes bored into hers.

'Some of them,' Alana admitted. 'Questioning someone like Bessie, even about what she might have had for breakfast, can make her more confused. In Eight B we've usually got at least two, sometimes up to five dementia patients at any one time. There's a dementia ward, but it hasn't enough beds, and so it's used primarily for younger people with early onset Alzheimer's, when they reach the stage their family can't keep them at home. Our patients are usually admitted with other problems as well, and require the attention of specialists who come here but don't regularly visit the dementia ward. So, really, the patients need to be here.'

The blue eyes studied her as if trying to assess something behind her words, then he gave a little nod.

'OK, I can understand what you're saying, but these students are our doctors of the future, and I've always believed they should see and understand the progress of patients from their entry through A and E to their discharge.'

'What they should see and understand is that patients are people!' Alana muttered. 'Students come in here with their white coats and officious attitudes which I know are usually caused by nerves. But they are so obviously expecting answers to the questions they ask that the patients try to please them. Then the students leave, laughing before they're even out of the ward about the old codger who thought his leaky mitral valve had something to do with his bladder. It's their attitude I object to.'

'Me, too!'

She was so startled by his agreement she looked up to see him watching her, a slightly puzzled frown drawing his finely shaped eyebrows together.

'That's part of what I'm hoping to achieve by introducing them to the admissions ward.'

Alana shook her head, not certain she was hearing right.

'It's what you're hoping to achieve?' she repeated, then, because it seemed impossible, she added, 'How?'

'By getting them to dig deeper, to draw up patient profiles as part of their studies. To look at the whys of illness, and the demographics of hospital patients. Later on in their training, particularly in their intern year, they're too busy to think beyond the very next minute, but if they've had early training in seeing patients as people, a little of that should remain.'

He smiled at her before adding, 'That's the phrase I use as well—see patients as people first!'

The smile was so unexpected, and lit up his face so vividly, she had to blink away the brilliance. But blinking had no effect on the melting sensation the smile had caused in her bones.

Melting bones and Rory Forrester? Oh, no, definitely not! she told herself as he moved to a phone on the other side of the horseshoe of desks to respond to a page. They might both be in agreement over the 'patients as people' issue, but she doubted whether the students would change their ways, and she knew she would still have to fight him over it.

She had also, rationally and carefully, worked out that love, should it come, would grow out of friendship, and mutual respect, and a host of other practical things that had nothing to do with melting bones.

Melting bones were signs of lust, and lust only led to dangerously unsatisfactory relationships.

Hello, Alana! First you're stuck on a profile you see in a dark theatre for a few minutes—and perhaps the dry-cleaning fluid in his suit—now, two days later, your thoughts are leaping from lust to relationship with a man you've only just met? A man who is probably married. A man you're prepared to fight on just about every issue he wishes to pursue.

A man who uses a bone-melting smile as a weapon!

Puh-leese!

She slumped into a seat in front of the computer, trying to concentrate on work—and wondering, as she often did, when work, i.e. nursing, had turned into a computer-based career. Bessie Oliver… She checked the latest info from the social work department—possibility of a bed at a nursing home, miles from where the woman currently lived with her granddaughter.

Alana phoned Prue.

'I really don't want her to have to go. She'll hate it. You know how she is in hospital—always wanting to go home.'

'But, Prue,' Alana said gently, 'the home she wants to go to isn't your place anyway. It's the home where she grew up. Wherever she goes isn't going to be that particular home. So, really, it's up to you. Would visiting her at Belltree Gardens be possible for you?'

'I guess so. It's a fair drive but once I've got the kids in the car an extra twenty minutes doesn't really matter. And I could visit at night sometimes when Bart's at home to mind them.'

Alana was about to give a thumbs-up of triumph when Prue spoke again.

'But I feel terrible about it, and if I go to visit her and see she's unhappy, I'll feel worse. I promised Mum I'd look after her.'

Alana sighed, but not so Prue could hear her.

'How about you go and look at Belltree? Today if possible. I'll lie and say we're definitely taking the bed, because if we hesitate someone else will snap it up. But, remember, look at the place from the point of view of how it's kept, whether the staff seem cheerful and competent, if the patients seem tidy and well cared-for. Bessie isn't going to be really happy anywhere, I think you know that. What you've got to consider is whether she'll be looked after as well as you can do it, or not.'

There was silence for a moment, then Prue conceded her point.

'I'm not doing it very well at the moment,' she admitted. 'And you're right about her not being really happy anywhere. But it's so sad—so pathetic really. She was such a vibrant, intelligent woman and she'd hate to think she'd lost her dignity the way she has.'

'But she doesn't realise it,' Alana assured the worried woman, crossing her fingers behind her back, because sometimes she wondered if dementia victims actually were aware of what they'd lost.

'Telling lies?' a fast-becoming-familiar voice murmured, and fingers lightly flicked against hers.

Alana stiffened, partly because the slight and fleeting touch had produced a reaction more in keeping with being prodded by a red-hot wire and partly because she'd been caught out in such childish behaviour.

By a man with whom she'd barely drawn up battle lines.

Somehow, she finished her conversation with Prue, then she turned to where Rory Forrester was leafing through the patient list.

With his profile clearly lit by light from a window beyond him.

CHAPTER THREE

ALANA'S heart thudded to a halt, then resumed beating, but erratically.

It couldn't be! And even if it was, you can't fall in love with a profile. You settled all of that. And all the girl talk about Mr Tall, Dark and Handsome taking the seat beside hers at the concert had been just that—girl talk!

Fantasy!

And it was dark in the theatre—how do you know it was the same profile? Rory Forrester obviously hasn't recognised you!

'Is this a fairly typical Eight B population?' he asked, and, realising she was still holding the receiver in her hand while her mind whirled confusedly along foggy byways, she set it carefully back in its cradle and tried desperately to understand his question.

He waved the list towards her.

She straightened her spine, told herself she knew the answers and that, of course, her lips and tongue would still work no matter what her heart was doing, then answered—carefully.

'I haven't checked the details of every patient on the list today, but we usually have about six to eight patients with pneumonia query chest infections, about four patients with other infections—bladder infections or cystitis being the most common of them—then always a couple of badly ulcerated wounds—usually on legs.'

She frowned as he flipped the page over.

'You probably realise a lot of our patients are elderly and many of them have been living on their own or with equally elderly partners. They manage daily tasks just fine, and the majority of them lead full and interesting lives, but they haven't grown up in a ''seeing the doctor'' culture and tend to let minor irritations, like a sore leg or a bad cough, go for a while until the infection reaches the stage where only hospitalisation and IV antibiotics will help.'

'I do realise that,' the man said calmly, while his eyes told her to go teach her grandmother to suck eggs.

An overwhelming urge to hiss and spit at him crept over Alana and she knew exactly how Mrs Phillips's cat must feel.

'Dehydration, sometimes from an intestinal upset but also from a poor fluid intake, is also a common reason for admission.' Curbing the impulse to react, she continued her explanations—confining it to basics and hoping maybe she could bore him out of her space. 'Then stomach complaints themselves, if severe, and breathing problems—we generally have up to half a dozen asthma or emphysema patients at one time, and a range of query-type patients. Query kidney stones, query gallstones, query ulcerated intestines.'

She looked directly at him, ignoring the fact that the blue eyes were affecting her nearly as badly as the smile had earlier. Thank heavens the profile wasn't also on view.

It was because he was new, and she was worried about his effect on the running of the ward, that he disturbed her.

The physical reaction was simply an extension of that worry, and nothing at all to do with T-shirts kept in plastic bags.

'Does the ward work well?'

'Yes!'

Blunt answer to a blunt question, but then she remembered the days it didn't work well and felt compelled to elaborate.

'Most days!' she added. 'And when it doesn't, it's not the fault of the nursing or ancillary staff but the medical staff. We see a lot of specialist consultants, who are supposed to come in before their specialist outpatient appointments. I realise things happen and often they can't come, but at a certain stage during an unexpected call, or during their outpatients appointment list, they should have some idea of when they'll finish and be able to give us a rough idea of when they'll finally get here.'

The dark brows drew together.

'Why? So you can make sure the bed corners are all tucked in properly? Didn't that type of rigid inspection go out in the 'fifties or 'sixties?'

Alana hoped Rory Forrester could recognise a furious glare when he saw one.

'It's nothing to do with bed corners, although the sheets stay tauter and the patients are therefore more comfortable if the beds are properly made,' she snapped. 'It's to do with the patient and his or her family. The specialist makes the decisions about the patient's treatment, yet the patient and his or her advocates rarely get an opportunity to see the specialist. A visitor might, if he was lucky, get to see a junior doctor—someone who can't answer questions like ''How long will Grandma be in?'', ''What are you testing for now?'', ''Why choose this particular treatment?'' The interns and residents do their best, but most patients, or their advocates, want to see the boss.'

The mobile eyebrows rose.

'Really? It's been my experience that it's harder to interest the family—and often the patient as well—in the treatment and reasons for it than it is to get spare beds in the dementia ward. Most people simply don't care. They send Grandma to hospital and wait until they're asked to take her home.'

'What a revoltingly cynical attitude!' Alana snorted. 'Shows how rarely you specialists see real people—most of whom care a great deal for Grandma and want to understand what's wrong with her.'

She shrugged then added, 'Of course, once someone starts an explanation with a healthy injection of medical jargon, the listener can get lost, but that's the fault of the specialist, not the patient's relative or advocate.'

'Do I detect a note of antipathy towards specialists in your voice, Sister Wright? Is your opinion of their behaviour perhaps weighted by your own attitude?'

'If it is, it's an attitude developed through experience,' Alana told him. 'I've worked on this ward for seven years now, and believe I'm qualified to give an opinion about it.'

Rory Forrester gave her a slow smile, then raised an elegant, slim-fingered hand.

'Any number of opinions, apparently,' he murmured. 'On student rounds, length of patient stays, specialist visits…' He ticked off the list on his fingers. 'Have you any other issues you'd like to air?'

Supercilious attitudes might be one, Alana thought but a voice page was now summoning Dr Forrester to Ward Eight C, so she didn't get the opportunity to mention it.

He made polite apology noises and departed, leaving her feeling frustrated that she'd had the opportunity to speak to him yet had somehow been sidetracked so nothing had been resolved.

All in all, he was just as aggravating in person as she'd imagined he would be.

Though far better-looking than the photo in the staff newsletter had suggested.

Which led to her wondering if she'd kept a copy of that particular paper. She generally leafed through them then used them to line Stubby's litter tray, or shredded them for nests for Biddy. But because she'd known he was going to impact on her working life, she had a feeling she'd kept the issue.

She shuffled through the papers in her drawer but, apart from a few old and very squashed chocolate bars and half a packet of gum, nothing of any interest came to light.

Had someone pinned the photo on the ward noticeboard? Was that where she'd seen it recently?

She was about to hit herself on the head for even considering ways of sneaking it off the board when a voice, thankfully, interrupted her thoughts.

'You said Dr Wallace would be here by eight. I've already waited two hours.'

The justified complaint from a young wife anxious to see the specialist about her husband's kidney test results turned Alana's full attention back to work. Though she felt a momentary regret that Dr Forrester had left—she could have sicced this woman onto him!

'I'm sorry, Mrs Cheevers. Dr Wallace was expecting to do his round before he saw his outpatients, but he was unavoidably held up.'

Teeth gritted behind her false smile, she made a mental note of another aggravation she should bring up with Rory Forrester. Lying to protect the specialists who didn't let the ward know when they wouldn't be coming in.

'After all,' she fumed to Daisy, when she unexpectedly met her neighbour in the queue at the hospital canteen at lunchtime, 'all they have to do is phone the switchboard— or even get someone else to do it for them—and have an "I'm unavoidably delayed" message sent through to the ward. Is that so hard? Is politeness so old-fashioned now that no one cares?'

They shuffled forward, Daisy making noncommittal noises, which, now Alana thought about it, was Daisy's usual way of dealing with uptight friends.

'What are you doing here anyway? I thought you'd got rid of all your hospital sessions and were concentrating on your talk-back show, web site and books. Don't tell me you've left the talk-back show already?'

'No, but I'm thinking seriously about it—though I'd keep the web page going—and I have got rid of hospital sessions. But I still take on a few private patients and needed to talk to one of their— Oh, there he is. Over at the far table on the left. Rory Forrester. Have you met him yet? He's taken the flat above yours.'

Alana looked more closely at her friend. Daisy was the calmest, most placid person she knew. Verging on dead, she was so unemotional at times. Yet the disjointed explanation she'd just offered was not only flustered—it didn't make sense.

The pale green-grey eyes looked as limpid as usual, and the cloud of wild black hair wasn't obviously more dishevelled, yet the woman was definitely off balance.

Alana considered her own, momentarily, melting bones.

And the effect of the profile.

Did the man have some magnetic attraction for all women?

Did his body give off a scent like catnip, but, rather than it being specific for one woman, it attracted all woman as the plant attracted all cats?

Pleased by the idea it might not just be her who was thrown into a tizz by the man, she studied Daisy.

'Is he making your heart flutter?' she asked. 'Causing problems in your intestines? Is Daisy-who-doesn't-date about to become interested in a man?'

Daisy's laugh came so naturally, pealing out in sheer delight, that Alana was forced to believe her when she said, 'No way. He's a handsome enough man, but he's not pulling *my* strings. No, it's Jason who bothers me. He's been through such a lot, poor kid, and I can't do much to help until I know more background information.'

They'd reached the checkout and, after handing over a note to cover the cost of her lunch, Daisy turned apologetically to Alana.

'Normally I'd ask you to join us—particularly as we're all neighbours. But I really do need to discuss Jason and it wouldn't be right...'

'Of course not,' Alana assured her, waving her on her way, but as Daisy crossed the room to Rory Forrester's table, Alana's eyes followed her while her mind went on a rampage, fitting bits and pieces of information together and not liking the whole picture one little bit.

Daisy was seeing a Jason. Alana's Jason?

Well, she'd kind of established Jason lived in Near West so, if he was seeing a psychologist, Daisy would be handy for him to visit.

But if Jason was the same Jason, and he belonged to Rory Forrester, then not only was Rory Forrester going to be a presence in her life at work but he was living in her building. Actually, Daisy had said that as well.

Rory Forrester in her building...

Profile, male scent and all!

She hauled her mind off the physical to concentrate on the clues.

The leasing of the flat then lack of habitation made sense—he'd disappeared from the hospital as well!

So where did that leave her?

Knowing he was married with a son—that's where that left her!

'Pay the lady and move on, please. You're holding up the queue.'

The demand from behind recalled her to where she was and, rustling hastily through her purse, she found change, paid her bill, then carried her tray across to a thankfully vacant table.

She sat down, conscious of a heaviness inside her chest, as if something she'd been looking forward to had proved a disappointment, or a longed-for event had been cancelled.

Ridiculous! she told herself. She barely knew the man, and didn't like what she did know of him, so finding out he was married didn't matter one jot.

Did it?

She remembered the cat—or, rather, something Jason had said about the cat. 'It was my mother's'. Was!

And Jason's introduction—such as it had been.

Hadn't he said his name was McAllister—or at least Mc-something?

Perhaps he used his mother's name.

Perhaps it's none of your business, she told herself in an effort to stem this tidal wave of supposition, none of which was getting her anywhere. It wasn't even particularly rational. Rory Forrester's private life was none of her concern.

In actual fact, his professional life, apart from when it impacted on Eight B, was also none of her concern.

She nodded to confirm she'd sorted that out, and tackled her lunch. If she hurried, she'd have time to duck down to the gym. While exercising after a meal wasn't ideal, she could lift weights for ten minutes and start getting back into nick, ready for the tennis season.

The note was on her desk when she returned. She stared at the unfamiliar writing, although the strong black slashes of the letters made her think immediately of Rory Forrester.

Using the tip of the nail on her forefinger, she pushed at the piece of paper, as if expecting it to explode. When it didn't, she left it on the desk but peered at it, in the end resorting to the glasses she hated to admit she needed in order to decipher the message.

Or try to decipher it!

The word 'mating' leapt out at her, but that was obviously because she was going a bit crazy and had male-female relationships on the brain. Maybe the word was 'meeting', for there seemed to be a time, '6 p.m.' after it. But the rest was as difficult to work out as a badly written prescription. At least with a script, if you knew the patient you could sometimes guess what might be prescribed—though she always phoned the writer to check before sending the order on to Pharmacy.

She gave in and picked up the note, holding it warily, as if something of the person who'd written on it might be transmitted through the paper.

As far as she could make out, Rory Forrester had called a meeting to discuss facelifts and some kind of presents in—she assumed the next word was 'hospital' because 'heaven' certainly didn't seem right—beds. The fact that the note was addressed to her—if she squinted her eyes the name could almost be taken for Wright rather than Witch—and that there was a time and a room number suggested she was being invited to join this discussion.

Finding his email address in the hospital directory, she sent an acceptance—only, she told herself, because she was curious to find out exactly what he wanted to discuss—and added that he might find emails easier for conveying messages than written notes.

Didn't say easier for whom, but she hoped he had enough intelligence, or had been told often enough by other recipients of his writing, to figure it out.

By the time her shift ended, she'd decided her best plan would be to go home, feed the animals, then come back to the hospital for the meeting. That way, if it ran late, she wouldn't be worrying. And, no, changing into civvies had nothing to do with her decision.

'Hey! Thought we might have a game.'

Jason was sitting on the front steps of the building, bouncing a ball up and down on his racket.

Have a game *and* feed the animals? If they had a game of tennis, there'd barely be time for a shower before she had to go back for the meeting. But the blue eyes watching her so closely had dark flecks in them and a darker ring around the iris. And the defiance, she was sure, was a cover-up for hurt of some kind.

A boy separated from his mother? Shifted against his will to a new home at a time when friends were all-important?

'OK,' she said, 'but only if you come up while I change and start on my chores for me. You can wash Stubby's water bowl and put out clean food and water for him—and do the same for the stray who eats off the veranda.'

For a moment she thought Jason was going to argue, but in the end he stood up and, though muttering slightly under his breath, followed her into the building.

Once inside the flat, she showed him where the various animal foodstuffs were kept and, when he was diverted by the special prescription marsupial powder, promised to explain it to him some other time.

'Tonight?' he said hopefully. 'The DM's got a meeting and I'm ordering pizza. I could get some for you. Have it delivered here.'

He sounded so eager, Alana hated to deny him.

'Sorry—I've got a meeting as well,' she said, wary about mentioning with whom in case that upset Jason even more. 'But another night—or if you want to eat late, I should be home by eight at the latest.'

Jason shrugged.

'*He* said he'd be home by then as well,' he muttered, decorating the 'he' with a shovel-load of resentment.

Alana shook her head and excused herself to get changed. Rory Forrester's relationship with his son was none of her business, but from the way Jason talked, it would take a lifetime of seeing Daisy to sort the poor kid out. Though maybe the father should be seeing someone as well, someone who could teach him how to get on better with his son.

When she came back out, Jason was tempting the guinea-pig babies with a piece of apple.

'I noticed it all cut up in your fridge,' he said. 'I thought it might be for them.'

'For their mother and the rabbit mostly,' Alana said, 'but the babies have to learn to eat solids sometime so it's good to offer it to them.'

She grabbed her racket out of the hall closet, checked he had balls, and was about to leave the flat when she remembered she didn't have keys. Jason was stroking one of the baby guinea pigs through the wire of the cage.

'I'll show you how to pick them up, and also how to clean their cages. If you're looking for an after-school job, I could really do with some help looking after them all.'

His face lit up as if she'd offered him a precious gift.

'Do you mean it?' he asked with such intensity she wondered who'd made offers in the past then not followed through.

'Of course I mean it,' she assured him. 'I've got a spare front-door key that I had cut when I lost mine. I'll give it to you so you can come and go when it suits you. Gabi up on Four also has a spare key of mine, so if you misplace yours any time, and she's at home, you can borrow hers.'

Again she read something in his face—surprise, but a wary look as well, as if he was always prepared for life to not live up to his expectations. It reinforced her decision to put her trust in him. She'd found, with animals, if you showed you trusted them, they usually reciprocated.

Well, most of them did.

And if she wanted to prove trust, now was the time to do it. She fished the key out of the bottom of an empty vase and passed it to Jason, smiling to herself as he tucked it carefully into his pocket then smoothed the Velcro fastening to make sure it couldn't fall out.

They walked down the stairs, and out to the court.

'Best of three?' Jason suggested, and Alana checked her watch.

'If we've time,' she told him. 'I can play till five-thirty at the latest.'

Jason nodded, and offered her the serve.

It was a good game, but this time he was prepared for her ability and fought tenaciously for every point. When the third set went to a tie-break, and her watch said five-forty, she knew she had to stop.

'We'll call it a draw,' she said to him, and saw shadows

chase across his face. Easy-to-read shadows, like resentment and anger. 'Don't try the dirty looks on me,' she warned him. 'I said I'd play till five-thirty and I've already gone an extra ten minutes.'

He seemed taken aback, but in the end conceded her point with an abrupt nod.

'I'll have a hit against the wall,' he said. 'Could you show me where the lights are?'

Alana turned on the lights for him, reminding him to make sure the gate locked behind him when he left.

'I should be home by four tomorrow,' she said, 'but to be on the safe side, why don't you come down at five? I'll show you the routine with the animals.'

Jason stared at her as if he had no idea what to make of her—as if, having upset her, he could expect no further friendship.

Boy, was Daisy going to have her work cut out with this kid.

She smiled as she said goodbye, but in her head she was arguing that it wasn't up to Daisy to help the boy—well, not entirely up to Daisy. It was Rory Forrester who should be providing stability in his son's life, so Jason had a solid and secure base behind him as he ventured through the wild-lands of adolescence.

She was late, of course, by the time she reached the hospital, and finding that the room number she sought was, in fact, a student locker room, she then had to make other guesses, eventually finding Rory Forrester in 47, a small meeting room on the fourth floor.

Fine, dark eyebrows rose at her late arrival, but she was damned if she'd apologise to him. Anyone who could make a figure four look like a nine didn't deserve an apology.

Sinking into the closest seat, she found herself next to Ted Ryan, the registrar in Internal Medicine, so virtually the 2-I-C to Rory Forrester. Beyond Ted, Alana could see two residents and a couple of interns, and scattered in amongst them a number of senior nurses, no doubt the charge nurses of other wards under the senior physician.

'Ah, Sister Wright!' Rory Forrester smiled genially at her. 'You know what the meeting's about?'

'Unless it's about facelifts and presents and beds in heaven then, no!' Annoyed at being singled out, Alana snapped out her reply, then enjoyed a moment of sheer delight as a bemused expression crossed his face. 'Your writing is more illegible than most doctors',' she added for good measure.

'But you'd have understood the emailed message, surely?' he said, recovering far too quickly and turning the tables on her.

'If I'd had time to read it,' Alana muttered to herself.

Ted Ryan patted her knee, more a calming than a comforting gesture she was sure—Ted having had experience of her temper.

Rory Forrester saw his registrar's hand move to Alana Wright's knee, and told himself that, far from feeling a brief stab of jealousy, he should be thankful she was involved with someone and get on with the discussion.

But wasn't Ted Ryan married?

He simply *had* to find time to go through the staff notes…

'We're actually discussing ways of facilitating student presence on the wards,' he said, addressing the words towards Alana but looking at a point beyond her head so he wasn't distracted by the way little bits of hair were escaping the plastic thingie in which she'd tried restraining it and curling beguilingly around her face.

'Like them or hate them, the students are here to stay, so let's see if we can come out of the Dark Ages as far as their involvement is concerned, and put them to some use, so they're contributing something while they learn.'

He went on to explain his idea on having them draw up patient profiles, his eyes straying back towards the latecomer, probably because he'd already mentioned this to her.

Alana caught his look and wondered if he was expecting a response.

'Will these profiles be used for anything?' she asked, only too happy to oblige as extra and unnecessary paperwork was another of her bugbears. 'Or are they just to keep the kids amused?'

The look he shot her way should have warned her but, once launched, she always found it hard to shut up.

'Don't we already have computer programs that extract patient profiles from the face sheets on patients' admittance forms? And will a patient profile make the person feel any better, or better inform him or her about his or her condition?'

She had plenty more to add but Rory Forrester's smile stopped her in her tracks.

'Are we doomed to argue throughout my tenure at Royal Westside, Sister Wright?'

'She can't help it,' Carole King, one of the other nurses, said. 'She'd argue underwater if she thought it would help her precious Eight B, and in a gag underwater if anyone dared to denigrate the place.'

The residents and other nursing staff laughed, while Ted gave her knee another calming—or warning—pat.

But it was too late for warnings.

'At least my passion is directed towards the patients rather than—'

Ted's fingers dug sharply into her leg and she swallowed the words 'senior O and G consultant' that she'd been about to fling at Carole.

Ted was right. The entire hospital might know about Carole's and Bill's affair, but it was hardly appropriate to bring up in a staff meeting.

And it was so unlike her usual philosophy of live and let live, Alana decided, that until she'd worked out why

Rory Forrester had such an unsettling effect on her, she'd better sit still and shut up.

'Thanks,' she whispered to Ted, patting the hand still resting on her leg.

Definitely married. He'd been talking about his wife only this morning, Rory recalled, glaring at the couple playing handsies in the back row.

Somehow he got the meeting back on track, finally asking all present to put any ideas they might have for the useful occupation of med students in writing and email them to him.

'We've got to try to turn them from people most staff members see as nuisances into useful members of the hospital community.'

'Do you think he'd accept drug experimentation as a useful occupation?' Alana asked Ted, remaining seated beside him while the rest of the group shuffled hurriedly out of the room. 'Lobotomy trials? Sex changes?'

'For the person who prompted this meeting with her vocal complaints on the nuisance value of students, you're not coming up with much in the way of viable alternatives.'

The cool voice brushed like an icy wind change across the back of her neck. She'd watched Rory Forrester go out the door at the front of the room, but he'd apparently sneaked back in through the one she'd used and was now standing right behind her.

Listening to her 'bad taste' remarks.

Compelled by reasons she didn't want to consider right now, she turned towards him.

'As far as I'm concerned, the most useful thing they could do would be typing up the charts. At the moment, doctors' orders are still written on the paper charts on patients' beds, then later, one of the nursing or clerical staff types these orders and all the obs into the computer. If students did the typing—it could be done whenever they had time or on a roster basis or something—they'd be learning all about the patient, particularly if they have to check details from time to time, without bothering him or her with repetition of questions already asked.'

'Hell, Alana, I can think of a dozen issues that would prevent that,' Ted said, shaking his head over what he considered was stupidity. 'Confidentiality for a start.'

Alana laughed.

'You've got to be joking! I saw a report recently that stated at least seventy people within a hospital would see a supposedly "confidential" file. And that's only counting people who have a right to have it in their hands.'

'What about mistakes—typing errors?' Ted persisted, but Alana wasn't going to give in.

'They don't happen already? Tired staff members already make mistakes. Haven't you ever seen an "l" typed in instead of a "c" so it seems as if a patient has had two litres of drugs not two ccs?'

Rory Forrester laughed, a sound so unexpected that Alana was, at first, startled. But the laughter was genuinely full-blooded and carefree and she found herself smiling in response, though when he stopped for long enough to say, 'Carole was right. You'd argue in a gag,' she wasn't so sure she should be smiling.

'Come on, let's get out of here,' he added. 'Daisy Rutherford was telling me you're another inhabitant of the Near West complex. If someone as fit as you can walk slowly enough for an aching muscled wreck like me to keep up, I'll walk you home.'

Rory saw the startled expression on Alana's face, and an equally startled look on Ted's, but he told himself he was doing Ted's wife—and thus Ted himself—a favour, removing this woman from Ted's proximity.

The startled expression on Alana's face he'd think about later.

When he'd finished considering why he'd made the offer...

CHAPTER FOUR

BUT if Rory thought he might get to know Alana Wright a little better on the short walk home, he was doomed to disappointment. As they entered the lift, a stocky but handsome man greeted Alana with a demand to know what she was doing hanging around the hospital so late at night.

'Same as you, I imagine,' she said, smiling with obvious delight at the man. Did she flirt with every man in the hospital? Then, apparently remembering Rory's existence, she turned to him and said, 'Have you met the neighbour in the flat above yours? Alex Graham, works in ICU, specialising in Intensive Care. Alex, this is Rory Forrester— the phantom tenant of the third floor.'

Rory shook the hand Alex offered.

'I hadn't had time to move in before I was called away for a family emergency,' he explained. 'The Frosts kindly kept the flat vacant for me.'

Alex nodded.

'I know how family emergencies can throw you,' he said, with the kind of heartfelt empathy which made Rory feel the man really did know about such things. He then went on to ask Rory where he'd previously worked. And though Rory answered, part of him was wondering if this Alex Graham was now on his way home, and if walking Alana home was about to become a group endeavour.

More so than he'd thought, he realised when they walked out of the hospital building and were joined by an attractive woman who greeted Alex with a kiss and Alana with obvious delight.

More introductions—this time to Alex's wife, Gabi, who

56

had worked at Royal Westside but was now at the Children's Hospital across town.

He glanced towards Alana who didn't seem at all put out by these extra people joining them.

And why would she be? he demanded of himself. She thought him a nuisance and an interloper. She'd made that clear from the start.

But he felt thoroughly disgruntled as they strolled along the night-quiet streets, perfume from scented plants in residential gardens taking over from the exhaust fumes of the traffic.

'Nights like this when a number of us have been working late, we usually eat at Mickey's, the bar and bistro on the ground floor of Near West, but he's closed on Mondays so Alex and I are ordering in Chinese. Would you like to join us?'

Alana, walking with Alex directly behind Gabi and Rory, heard the question and held her breath. She was willing to admit to an inexplicable—if you ignored body scent—attraction to Rory Forrester, but she wasn't so sure she wanted to learn any more about him—stuff that would inevitably come out when Gabi began questioning him.

Gabi could worm the life history out of a—well, worm, probably—if given even the smallest window of opportunity.

'Thanks for the offer.' Rory's smile made Alana feel momentarily jealous of her lifelong friend. 'But I've a thirteen-year-old at home, and if he hasn't already ordered pizza, I've promised him he can.'

Alana saw Gabi's eyebrows rise and knew she was about to begin her oh, so subtle questioning, but Alex tapped her on the shoulder and the configuration of the group changed, so Alana found herself beside Rory.

'I've met Jason,' she said. 'I assume Jason's the thirteen-year-old you mentioned.'

Ha! Surprised him.

'You've met Jason?' he said, in such disbelieving tones that Alana felt what surely must be the things people called 'hackles' rise.

'Shouldn't I have?' she asked sweetly. 'And why's that? Was he under orders to stay shut in for three days?'

Rory's frown deepened, then, like sunlight coming out from behind a cloud, his eyes lit up and his smile washed the harshness from his face.

'He told you about the cat! You can't possibly be the tennis player?' he said. 'You? The Dragon Lady?'

He was so obviously delighted by this revelation Alana wanted to hit him, but as that wouldn't look good, she hit back instead.

'Well, I assume you're the Dungeon Master. I think that's a far worse name to be called. He only called me the Dragon Lady because I didn't let him win at tennis.'

He obviously wasn't put out by her reply, because the smile didn't seem to dim at all.

'Dragon Lady—Dungeon Master? What's all this?' Gabi asked. 'Some new game?'

Rory turned back towards her.

'My nephew, Jason, is living with me. He makes up names for people, and Alana and I were just commiserating with each other over his choices for us.'

'For us, huh?' Gabi murmured, directing both the words and another raised eyebrow in Alana's direction.

Alana, however, was too busy absorbing the 'nephew' part of the conversation. Maybe if Jason was his nephew, Rory didn't have a wife. Or even an ex-wife.

Well, not one with whom he shared a thirteen-year-old son.

And what's that to you? her head demanded.

They crossed the road and as they reached the Near West building Gabi, obviously not put off by Rory's polite refusal, said, 'If he hasn't eaten, we could order pizza for all

of us. I'd like to meet the boy game enough to call Alana
a dragon!'

'I'll see how he feels,' Rory said. 'We're both still ad-
justing to living together, so I try to let him be involved
with decisions. Mind you, when it comes to going to
school, it's a different matter. His decision on that one is
that it's a total waste of time.'

'I think we all feel that way at some time of our lives,'
Gabi said, then she nodded towards the building. 'Well, at
least he's home. The lights are on in your flat.'

Alana glanced up automatically and noticed that the
lights were also on in her flat. Had she turned them on
before she left?

Or maybe Jason had turned them on when he was feeding the animals.

The cats.

The others were, as yet, unfed!

Pleased to have an excuse to avoid Gabi's Chinese or
pizza party—and thus the possibility of spending more time
in Rory Forrester's company—she excused herself on the
grounds her pets needed attention and used the stairs up to
her floor.

As she put her key in the lock, she realised that, as well
as light, there was music flooding from her flat. A tremor
of uncertainty made her hesitate, but as burglars rarely
played music while they robbed and plundered, she opened
the door and was only half-surprised to find Jason sitting
happily in her favourite recliner, watching the music video
channel on pay TV and totally oblivious to her arrival.

'Hey!' she yelled, needing to raise her voice to get above
the music.

He shot out of the chair as if her voice had been a cattle
prod and turned, a little guiltily, towards her.

'I've just been sitting here. I haven't touched anything.
I really needed to escape,' he said, defiance vying with
hope in his eyes. 'My aunt arrived, the Dracula-clone

Drusilla. She's decided she wants to marry Rory, and thinks the way to hook him is by mothering me.'

He hesitated, looked away and added, 'I don't need another mother,' in so low a voice Alana barely heard it.

'I bet you don't,' she said, hoping she sounded less startled than she felt. 'But your uncle's just got home, and he'll be wondering where you are.'

'She'll tell him,' Jason said, the switch to cheerful and unrepentant so swift that Alana wondered how long he intended to stay.

'Perhaps you should still go home,' she suggested, not wanting to become involved in a family dispute.

The thin, not-yet-developed lips shut mutinously tight.

'She'd much rather I didn't. Being on her own with him will give her a chance for a bit of a snog with the DM.'

'Snog? What kind of word is that? I thought slang like that went out in the Dark Ages.' She grinned at him. 'Back when I was young!'

'My friend Peter says it's what his older brothers call all that kissing stuff,' Jason explained. 'Snogging, or tonsil tangoing—but that's so gross even thinking about it makes me want to puke.'

Me, too, when you put it like that, Alana thought, but as she suspected he was trying to divert her attention from the main point—his presence in her flat—with this teen-speak language lesson, she decided not to go into it.

'Well, whether he's snogging or not, you should still contact your uncle. Do you want to go up and speak to him, or use my phone?'

A sharp rap on the door saved Jason from making a decision, though from the look on his face he'd recognised the auditory signal. If she'd been wearing a voluminous skirt, he'd have hidden behind it.

Actually, she could have done with someone's skirt herself, she decided when a quick peek through the peephole revealed the man they'd both guessed it would be.

She opened the door wide enough to see out—but not wide enough to be an invitation.

'Is Jason here?'

Rory's demand was so peremptory—so ridged with anger—Alana's instinctive reaction was to close it again, but his foot reacted faster than her hand, effectively preventing her automatic response.

Then she had to pretend she hadn't been about to slam the door in his face, so she babbled out the first thing that came into her head.

'He's helping me feed the animals. I understood you knew where he was.'

'I was told!' Rory said, the words seething out through gritted teeth. 'Though no one mentioned feeding animals.'

Alana, aware from the scuffling noises behind her that Jason had made his way into the kitchen, let the door swing wider, revealing at least part of her menagerie in the form of the—to most people revolting—featherless parrot.

'What else beside apple for the guinea pigs?' Jason asked, right on cue, and Alana turned to shoot a 'don't overdo it' look at the little ham.

He was now smiling brightly at his uncle, as if both surprised and delighted to see him.

'Hi, Rory,' he said cheerfully. 'Did you see Drusilla? Wasn't that a nice surprise?'

Alana heard a noise that sounded like a low-pitched growl and, certain her latest uninvited guest couldn't be growling, looked around for the stray cat.

'Have you had anything for dinner? Did you order pizza?'

Maybe it *had* been him growling, she decided as the questions—fairly growly still—flew past her to Jason.

Who smiled benignly at his uncle and, with a hint of a conspiratorial wink at Alana, said, 'Well, no. I thought I might eat down here.'

Alana put up her hands.

'No way! Enough's enough, kid. I don't intend to be caught in the middle of whatever hassles you might be having with your uncle. And while I'm happy to have your help with the animals, and you're welcome to visit any time, you need to be asked to people's places for meals, not simply assume you can come as if it's your right.'

She saw disappointment flood his face and immediately felt like a traitor, then realised it was exactly how he'd intended her to feel.

'And don't try that ''poor me'' look, because it won't work.' She grinned at him. 'I'm the Dragon Lady, remember, so beware my fiery breath!'

She jerked her head towards the door and was surprised when he obeyed the unspoken instruction.

Even more surprised when he greeted his uncle with a complicated handshake that involved meshing of knuckles and much twisting of arms and slapping of palms. They must have some level of rapport—the boy and the Dungeon Master!

'Don't forget, I expect you at five tomorrow. I'll be doing my tri-weekly major house clean of all the animals' cages,' she told Jason, when he turned to say goodbye. 'Once I've shown you what's what, you can take over that job at the weekend.'

Rory opened his mouth as if he was about to say something, then closed it again, contenting himself with a nod of farewell.

Had he been going to object to Jason working for her? Alana wondered as she shut the door behind the pair.

Not that it mattered if he did object. The boy obviously needed plenty to occupy his time. She wondered what school he was attending, and if whatever school it was had regular after-school sporting activities.

And did he have a tennis coach? He was certainly good enough to be encouraged in the sport.

'Not that he's any of our business, is he?' she said to the

parrot, talking to the bird because the flat, all of a sudden, seemed very empty.

'Nor is his uncle,' she added to Biddy, who had obviously decided her babies were too old to feed and was pushing them towards the water dispenser in an attempt to get them drinking from another source.

But neither of these pieces of advice stopped her thinking about her neighbours on the floor above her. And about the woman called Drusilla, who'd arrived to 'snog' with Rory.

'Good luck to her,' Alana muttered savagely, setting about the tasks of cleaning the animals' feed and water bowls with unnecessary energy. She'd just completed her tasks when Gabi rang to enquire if she wanted to join them for Chinese.

'Rory Forrester has a visitor, and his nephew hasn't eaten, so they're all coming up. I've ordered extra—enough for a small army, according to Alex.'

The idea of playing 'happy tenants' with Rory, Jason and the dread Drusilla made Alana, to steal Jason's word, want to puke.

'Thanks but no thanks,' she told Gabi. 'I'm already so far behind in my chores the guinea-pig babies are eating their cage.'

But as she finished her tasks and made herself an omelette for dinner, her thoughts strayed to the fourth floor, and the people gathered in Gabi's flat.

All the people?

Alana arrived at work early the next morning, more anxious than ever to get on top of what was happening in the ward. If Rory could organise a staff meeting and actually have people turn up on what was virtually his first day in the hospital, then he was probably equally efficient at checking what was happening within his domain.

And doubtless the kind of man who was always on time.

'That'd be a nice change,' Will James remarked when

she ran into him a little later in the tearoom where both were grabbing a revivifying cup of coffee. 'I've had three complaints about Dr Wallace and his unreliability this week, and it's only Tuesday morning.'

'Coffee! I smell coffee. If someone would supply me with a cup—black and two sugars—I'll be their slave for life.'

'Be careful what you promise,' Will said, while Alana told herself it must be the fact she'd slept badly that had made her start at the sound of Rory's voice. 'Especially when Alana's closest to the urn,' Will added. 'She's not known for being kind to specialists.'

'No?'

Dark eyebrows rose and though Rory moved his lips in what could be taken—by someone who hadn't seen the real thing—to be a smile, the expression did nothing to lighten the lines of tiredness in his face or warm the greyness of exhaustion from his skin.

She passed him the coffee without comment, but Will wasn't so easily stopped.

'Bad night?' he asked, while Alana's imagination supplied her with vividly illustrated explanations of the specialist's lack of sleep.

'You could say that,' Rory said, blowing on the coffee then sipping cautiously.

He nodded, as if in thanks, to Alana, then said, 'I wanted to talk to you about Mrs Oliver. I was speaking to her—is it a granddaughter who looks after her?'

'Yes, Prue.'

'That's the one. Well, Bill Stevens, the O and G consultant, is apparently her specialist. I ran into him in the car park and he said he'd been wanting to talk to me. He doesn't think she can manage the grandmother any more, but he was saying there's a new hostel about to open which will have a secure residential area for Alzheimer's patients.

He apparently knows about it because he's on the board of the Alzheimer's Association…'

Rory looked up from his coffee to see Alana frowning at him, the expression so puzzling he completely lost his train of thought.

'What's wrong? What have I done now?'

The frown grew even fiercer, while the male nurse murmured, 'Uh-oh,' and left the room.

'You're not normal!' she said. 'Or is this just new-broom stuff?'

'Not normal? New broom?'

He heard his pathetic echo of her words, and regretted the impulse that had taken him into the tearoom, no matter how badly he'd needed the caffeine fix to help him over the stress and discomfort of the previous night.

'You're a specialist. You see the patients while they're here, do follow-up appointments if necessary, teach students, publish papers, maybe even do patient profiles, but specialists rarely get involved with the minutiae of patients' lives—in fact, I doubt most of them know anything about where or how their patients live.'

'That's a fairly sweeping generalisation, Sister Wright,' he said silkily. 'Based on your own years and years of experience?'

Her eyes narrowed.

'And that of other hospital staff,' she snapped. 'OK, you get a lot of good ones—people like Josh Phillips who goes out of his way to include the whole family in his treatment of a child—but up in Eight B the patients are little more than bed numbers. Take Dr Wallace. He didn't turn up at all yesterday, and this morning, when, according to his secretary, he'd definitely be doing an early round at seven-thirty he hasn't been sighted.'

'Dr Wallace?'

'The renal specialist. I've a number of patients under him. They see a resident and occasionally his registrar might drop in, but it's not the same, although I guess most of them don't realise the registrar's not the boss.'

She paused long enough to take a deep breath, then continued her complaint against the errant specialist.

'But the people who do know—the ones who actually want to see him so they can ask questions—get upset, not with him because he's not here but with my staff for saying he will be.'

Her indignation had brought colour to her cheeks, and the spark of battle in her smoky blue-grey eyes.

'Is he the only culprit—the reason you've painted all specialists so black?'

The frown returned.

'Dr Curtis, the thoracic specialist, is supposed to do visits once a week. I think the last time we saw him was a month ago.' She paused and looked into Rory's eyes. 'I don't mind specialists ignoring the ward—after all, most are over-extended as it is, and their registrars or residents do a fine job. What I do object to is them saying they'll come and then not turning up. At least if I know they're not coming, I can advise family members who wish to speak to a particular specialist to phone him in his rooms.'

'And does that work?' Rory asked, aware he should be doing his own ward rounds, not chatting to Alana in the tearoom. 'My experience of phoning specialists has always prompted a high level of frustration and, no doubt, contacting me is just as bad.'

'I don't care if it works or not,' Alana told him, the dark-lashed eyes daring him to argue. 'At least that way it's his receptionist or secretary copping the abuse, not my staff.'

'Ah!'

The sound was so replete with understanding Alana peered suspiciously at him.

'What's that supposed to mean?'

His eyes widened innocently, then a real smile, albeit a tired one, appeared.

'Your last sentence explained so much. I did wonder why a woman like yourself, who doesn't hesitate to speak her mind to mere specialists—I've seen you in action, remember—should be so hung up over their behaviour. It's your protective instincts coming to the fore—you want to tuck all the staff under your sheltering wing. I should tell Jason to rename you Mother Hen.'

He hesitated, then added, 'Thank you for your kindness to Jason, by the way. He's been through a difficult time and it's made him prickly and defensive, but underneath the prickles there's a good kid.'

'And *I'm* a mother hen?' Alana teased, turning away from him to rinse out her cup. 'Are you finished with the coffee?'

She swung back to take his cup, adding, 'I'm also a slave-driver. If you're here to do a round, let's go.'

He handed her the cup, his fingers touching hers, quite by accident, in the exchange, yet the charge he could generate with his smiles shot through her once again at this physical connection and she had to remind herself that love was something which grew slowly—out of friendship and mutual respect and affection.

Not physical reactions or psychic manifestations of body odour!

Which obviously wasn't mutual as he had no idea she'd sat next to him at the theatre.

If it had been him...

'This conversation started with Bessie Oliver. Am I to do something about contacting the new hostel, or will the O and G man speak to Prue?'

Rory, who'd been enjoying the relaxing qualities of coffee and a chat with Alana, wondered what had swung the mood in the room so unequivocally back to work.

Did she time her coffee-breaks?

He hadn't seen her looking at her watch.

'Bill will speak to the granddaughter. Had you found anywhere else?'

'A possible placement in a nursing home a fair distance from Prue's home. It wasn't ideal but might have done.'

Alana sounded as if 'might have done' wasn't really good enough, and he wondered if she expected perfection of herself all the time. She obviously expected it of her specialist colleagues.

Including him?

He heaved his tired, aching body upright—he was too damn old to be sleeping on a couch, but Drusilla's offer that he share his own bedroom with her had been fraught with too many dangers to even consider—and followed Alana out of the room. His mood brightened perceptibly as he admired the way her lithe body moved beneath the Royal Westside nurse's uniform of slim-fitting navy trousers or skirt—she was in trousers today—and bluey-green coloured top, the style varying, he thought, according to seniority.

He rolled his eyes in horror that he could even be considering the attraction of a woman's body movement. He had enough woman problems with Drusilla around!

But as he accompanied Alana around the ward, meeting all the new patients—not just those he might see more of later in the internal medicine ward—he found himself admiring more than the way Alana Wright moved. Without being sugar sweet—he couldn't imagine her ever managing that—she gave the impression of being deeply interested in every person under her care, and made it obvious that, even if they were only temporarily on her ward, they were still deserving of every attention she and her staff could provide.

And the patients responded, he realised when he stopped to explain to Mrs Armstrong that he'd scheduled her for an endoscopy later in the day. She'd immediately turned to Alana for support.

'That's the test I had last time, isn't it?' she enquired.

'Where I had to swallow the tube? Will I come back here after it?'

'That's up to Dr Forrester,' Alana told her. 'If he finds bleeding polyps and can stop them bleeding while he's fiddling around inside your stomach, then you can probably come back here for an hour or so to get over it and then go home. But if he finds anything else...'

She nodded to Rory, finally deferring to him.

'I may need to keep you in for further treatment, either more extensive cauterisation or, as a last resort, surgery—though that isn't too fearsome these days with all the new techniques.'

Mrs Armstrong beamed at him.

'I'm sure you'll do whatever's right,' she said, causing Alana, as they moved away, to mutter, 'You do have a way with women, don't you?'

But it wasn't this barbed comment he remembered after the round finished but her attitude to her patients. He found himself comparing it, later in the day, with the staff in other wards. Not that the other staff were any less effective, or even less compassionate.

Just not as *involved* somehow.

Actually, she was the kind of charge nurse he'd like to see down on the gastroenterology ward, where most of his patients would be admitted.

The thought had no sooner surfaced than he smiled to himself. He could just imagine Alana's reaction to that suggestion. Even before he'd met her, he'd heard about the woman who considered Eight B her own personal fiefdom, defying anyone to consider it less important than any other ward in the hospital.

Alana was pleased when Rory finally departed, but her nerves stayed twitchy, as if poised to spring into reactive mode should he make an unexpected reappearance. She told them this was unlikely—he'd already spent more time in Eight B in two days than past senior physicians spent in two weeks—but she was beginning to realise her nerves had developed a way of ignoring her advice.

Keeping busy was one answer. With four patients either going home or being transferred, she had to prepare for four new admissions already waiting downstairs then, later in the day, find room for another three, doubling up the beds in a couple of single-bed rooms on a temporary basis.

Mrs Armstrong, polyps successfully cauterised, returned as Alana was going off duty and, announcing that the lovely Dr Forrester had said she could go home, promptly packed her bag and, once through the discharge procedure, was heading home to Alf.

'Will someone come for you?' Alana asked. 'Shall I phone your neighbour—Jenny, isn't it?'

Mrs Armstrong shook her head.

'The nurse in Recovery phoned the volunteer driver service and Jack's available to take me home.'

Was it still the blood transfusion making Mrs Armstrong's cheeks look so rosily pink, or was the colour connected to a slight tremor in her voice when she'd mentioned the volunteer driver's name?

'He heard from Jenny I was here and came to see me last night,' the older woman confessed. 'Said he'd probably be around later today if I needed someone to drive me home.'

Alana felt her heart lift at the woman's shy but obvious delight. People talked about first love being memorable, but to find love late in life must surely be even more magical.

She was still thinking about it as she walked home, and was smiling to herself as she unlocked her door so, of course, Daisy, coming out as she was going in, caught her foolishness.

'Good day?' Daisy teased.

'Not bad, but I was thinking about love,' Alana explained.

'Not you, too!' Daisy said. 'It's been like an epidemic

in the place the last few months. Even Philip, one of the dentists downstairs, has fallen—apparently for a patient with perfect molars.'

'Yuck! How revolting!' Alana grimaced at the thought. 'But if you must know, I remain immune.' Almost immune? 'I was thinking of a patient, and finding love late in life. Mrs Armstrong was definitely blushing, as if just saying the man's name raised her body temperature. Do you think love or attraction, or whatever it is, feels the same at any age?'

'I can't see why not,' Daisy replied. 'There are theories about the stages of love and its effect on people. I know some people believe love between the age of thirty and forty is different—and usually life-altering. How old's your Mrs Armstrong? If she's older than that, I could look up a few books and see what I can find about later romances.'

Alana chuckled.

'They might not go up to the decade of the nineties,' she said, 'which is where Mrs Armstrong fits.'

'Oh, how lovely!' Daisy couldn't contain her delight and clapped. 'What a treat to feel the thrill of love again at that age.'

They chatted a little longer, but it was that remark—or more the word 'thrill'—which remained with Alana after they'd parted.

She knew what Daisy meant by the word—the tingly physical response that was a strange blend of extreme excitement and a wary apprehension. But wasn't that kind of thrill a purely physical response? More to do with lust than love?

Which raised another question. Would ninety-something-year-olds go pink with lust?

The parrot's greeting reminded her she had more to do than consider the implications of lust in nonagenarians. Jason would arrive shortly, and she had to make sure she had enough paper for new nests for her pets. Most of her neighbours kept clean paper for her and she collected masses of it at work. All of this was shredded to provide the animals with fresh paper three times a week.

She was still shredding when Jason arrived and, pronouncing himself delighted with the working of her very basic shredder, took over the job. Then Alana showed him her routine, and told him about the baby marsupials she sometimes looked after, tiny kangaroos or wallabies mostly, their mothers having been killed by cars.

'Because they're allergic to cow's milk, we use the special formula. I'm part of a large group who voluntarily care for injured native animals, but I'm not often called on to take babies because there are others who specialise in them.'

'I've seen the signs by the roadside with phone numbers for people to call if they find an injured animal.'

Jason's face, when he was interested and animated, showed signs of the very good-looking man who'd eventually emerge from the chrysalis of adolescence. A good-looking man not unlike his uncle.

Alana switched her thoughts back to the explanations.

'That's the group I belong to,' she said. 'When I do have one of these very young and very dependent creatures, Madeleine Frost up on the top floor takes it during the day, because at a young age the animals need at least hourly feeds, and I do nights.'

'I could help,' Jason offered, and Alana laughed as she lifted the parrot out of his cage, setting him on the back of a chair while she cleaned.

'Perhaps when you're on holidays you can help Madeleine with the day feeds, but I can't imagine your uncle being too pleased if I got you into a job that required waking up on the hour every hour all night long. You'd fall asleep at school.'

'School's not so important!' Jason muttered, the anger

she always sensed in him returning at this slight provocation.

'Not if you're going to be a layabout all your life,' Alana agreed, and saw his eyes spark with more emotion.

'I'm not. I'm going to be a tennis professional,' he told her, familiar eyes defying her to argue.

'That's good, but it makes school even more important. You've no idea the number of sports stars who are ripped off by their management because they don't understand the basics of business and investment.'

'Really?' Jason asked, lifting the now clean parrot cage from her hands and hanging it back up. He spread the paper he'd cut to size in the bottom, then he lifted the bag of sand and waited for her nod before sprinkling a heavy layer over the paper. 'Why would people do that?'

The question came so long after the remark she had to think back to what she'd said.

'I guess they only do it if they think they can get away with it, but I guarantee that at least once a month there's an article in the newspaper about a sportsperson splitting with his or her management, or even taking court action against their former management.'

'So I'd have to keep an eye on what they did with my money?'

Alana hid a smile at the confidence of youth.

'Yes, and read all the papers they give you to read and definitely, and most importantly, read any contract before you sign it. And if you don't understand it, ask someone you trust. Your uncle, perhaps.'

'Or Rosemary,' Jason said. 'She's a lawyer.'

Assuming Rosemary was another aunt, Alana kept working, showing Jason how to check the water dispensers were functioning in all the cages, where the kitty litter was kept, and how to double-bag all the rubbish, then tie it securely before dumping it in the bins downstairs.

Once done, she smiled at him.

'Well, I suppose after all that work, I could ask you to stay to dinner,' she said. 'I was going to barbeque some steak on the balcony. That sound all right to you?'

Jason nodded, then said, 'But I'd better check with the DM first. With Drusilla around, he might need me to block the chances of a snogathon!'

He grinned as if remembering her distaste for the word, then with a 'Back in a minute!' he disappeared out the door.

Alana's immediate reaction was regret for possibly giving Rory the opportunity for a snogathon, but she dismissed that as unworthy. Jason deserved a treat.

'I'll just try not to think of the snogathon!' Alana muttered to herself as she headed to the bathroom for a quick shower before tackling the preparations for dinner.

CHAPTER FIVE

THE knock on the door came while Alana was still in the shower. Without bothering to dry herself, she dragged on her towelling bathrobe to go and let Jason in.

But the peephole revealed the uncle, not the boy.

Great! I open the door and he sees me dripping water, tangled hair, total mess, which shouldn't matter but *does*, or I don't open the door and antagonise him totally as he must know I'm in here because Jason will have just spoken to him.

She opened the door.

'Yes?'

Rory had the hide to smile!

'I'm not selling anything,' he said, obviously responding to her abrupt, putting-off-a-salesperson tone. 'But I was walking home and it struck me that, as a tennis player, you might know a good coach. Jason went to the Rosedale Tennis Academy in Sydney but he stopped playing a couple of months ago so I didn't get a chance to ask anyone there for a recommendation up here.'

'You were walking home? Just now? You haven't seen Jason?'

Alana forgot her general dampness as she tried to assimilate this new conversation, but Rory interrupted before she made the switch.

'Seen Jason? Why? What's wrong?' He grasped her arm as if willing, if necessary, to shake answers out of her, and though she thought this reaction—as close to alarm as Rory was likely to show—was a bit over the top, she answered quickly.

75

'Nothing's wrong with Jason. It's just that I was expecting him, not you.'

Blue eyes raked over her, from the top of her head to
the tip of her bare and still wet toes, then back up again.
The shapely dark eyebrows rose.

And with them Alana's temper.

'I'm not into corrupting minors, if that's what you're
thinking, Dr Forrester. I was in the shower when you
knocked.' She snapped the words at him, wondering if ir-
ritation was a byproduct of attraction. 'We've been cleaning
out the animal cages. He went home to ask if he could stay
for dinner.'

'You've invited him this time?' The eyebrows rose
again.

'Why not? Do you object?'

Rory studied the prickly, antagonistic—not to mention
wet—woman in front of him. What was it about her that
got under his skin? Apart from the fact she was very attractive, of course. And what was it about him that always
seemed to anger her?

Maybe she was just naturally bloody-minded, which
would explain why she was still single and apparently un-
attached at thirty. The not-so-subtle interrogation at the
Grahams' the previous evening hadn't been all one-sided!

Yet she'd been kind to Jason...

Which raised the question of why, when he should be
thanking heaven on bended knee that Jason had found a
friend, he felt resentful?

He saw the impatience gathering in her eyes, and remembered she'd asked a question.

Maybe more than one.

Definitely one about whether he objected to the lad having dinner with her.

'No, he can come to dinner if you really want him, but
don't let him become a nuisance to you,' he said, and hoped
it was an OK answer. Then, because he couldn't tell from

her expression whether it was or not, he found himself speaking again. 'Gabi and Alex were telling me about Mickey's Bar and Bistro. Could I buy you dinner there on Friday night? As a thank-you for being kind to Jason? We could talk about tennis coaches then.'

Various expletives sounded in Rory's head as he heard himself issue this half-baked invitation. For a start he had enough 'woman trouble' with Drusilla's arrival, so getting involved—even at the basic level of a thank-you dinner— with another one—particularly one to whom he rather thought he was attracted—was tempting fate.

He was wondering how he could sort this out when Alana did it for him.

'I am not "being kind" to Jason, as you put it. He's a friend—or at least an acquaintance who's likely to become a friend. As for needing a reward like being taken out to dinner—that's ridiculous. You can't pay people for being friends.'

Her eyes, more grey than blue this evening, sparked with anger and a faint flush was visible beneath the lightly tanned skin on her cheeks, while her pale-knuckled grip on the door suggested she was only just holding back from slamming it in his face.

Great! He'd asked, and she'd refused, so that was that. No more obligations, no potential problems—so why was he running off at the mouth, still talking, practically persuading...?

'I'm sorry. I put that badly. And I do want to talk about a tennis coach—and maybe a club, and whatever else he'll need.' Frustration with the situation—this woman, Jason, his life in general—made him sigh and he ran his fingers through his hair, remembering a haircut was one more minor thing he had to somehow fit into his life.

'Damn it all, just come to dinner with me, won't you? Is that too much to ask?'

Her eyes narrowed but he noticed her grip on the door

had relaxed and he suspected there might even be a smile lurking around her lips.

'Put like that, it's an invitation that's hard to refuse,' she said, letting just a hint of laughter flirt around her lips. 'But aren't you forgetting Jason, and your visitor—his aunt, isn't it?'

'How can I possibly forget my visitor when every bone in my body is complaining after one night on the couch? As for Jason, he's my sole concern, apart from work, and even that would have to take a back seat to his welfare if any more disasters occur. So asking you out to dinner, Dragon Lady, is not a date or anything even resembling a date. It's a request for help on a night when Drusilla has already arranged to take Jason to the movies.'

Alana heard the words, and though there was no mistaking the central message—dinner but not a date—they raised so many other queries she'd probably have to eat with him every night for a week if she wanted to find out the answers.

But she could start with one night.

'I guess it would give us an opportunity to talk about a few things,' she conceded. 'We haven't really resolved the student issue, and Ted tells me you're starting student rounds on Monday.'

His quick frown appeared, as if just talking about the students irritated him, but if he wanted her help with getting Jason settled, the least he could do—

'Bargaining with me, Sister Wright?' he asked, interrupting her thoughts, the frown replaced by a smile. 'When you've just finished telling me one shouldn't expect payment for being friends?'

The shift in his mood was disconcerting enough, but at the same time he leaned slightly towards her, as if drawn by some immutable force. For one riveting moment she thought he was going to kiss her.

And for one cataclysmic moment, she actually considered kissing him back.

Time expanded, stretched impossibly, imploded into nothingness, and the moment passed.

Alana felt heat rise in her body and willed it not to reach her cheeks, then, in case it did, tried a diversion.

'We've got right off the subject of this evening's dinner. Is it OK for Jason to have dinner here? Actually, it's a wonder he hasn't given up on you and come down anyway.'

Rory nodded as if acknowledging her tactics—and possibly something else—agreed that his nephew could eat with her and said goodbye.

Alana, now air-dried, shut the door and leaned against it.

Had she agreed to have dinner with him on Friday night or not? She rather thought she had.

But where did he get off inviting her like that? As if he assumed she'd have nothing better to do on a Friday night.

Which she didn't, but that wasn't the point.

Friday night?

This Friday night?

She clapped her hands to her temples and began to massage the headache she was certain would erupt any minute.

Of course she had something better—no, not necessarily better, just something else—to do on Friday night! In the panic which had followed the silly attraction attack last Saturday night—and the man still hadn't recognised her—she'd emailed Jeremy and suggested meeting him at Mickey's for a drink. It was the perfect venue for meeting a stranger as a number of her friends were likely to be there, so if Jeremy turned out to be an axe murderer she'd be safe.

Now—massage, massage—she'd have to tell Rory that she couldn't have dinner with him on Friday and there was no way in the world he'd believe the truth—that she couldn't make it because she *did* have a prior engagement.

Take me out and shoot me now!

The massaging wasn't helping much, so she tried a groan, and although that eased a minuscule amount of tension from her chest, it made so little difference to her overall condition she didn't bother trying it again.

Another knock on the door—Jason for sure, this time— put paid to having an immediate nervous breakdown, but mindful of Rory's look when she'd greeted him in her bathrobe, she called out, 'Just a minute.' Then scuttled into her bedroom to drag on some underwear and a long straight house-dress, which, though split to the knees up each side, was cover enough to satisfy even the most censorious of uncles.

She let Jason in, suggested he help himself to either juice or soft drink from the fridge, then, realising the sooner she contacted Rory the better, opened her mouth to ask for their phone number.

She closed it again when she considered the implications of the question. Jason, being a teenager, would want to know why, and instinct told her he might not like the idea of her having dinner with his uncle—even when she wasn't—particularly not when it was to discuss him. Jason him, not Rory him!

Maybe groaning *would* help!

'And could you pull the meat—it's in the pack marked "Eye Fillet" in the meat tray—out for me, please. I just need to make a phone call.'

She dashed into the bedroom and phoned Madeleine Frost, who, in between yelling at her twin boys—it must be the nanny Ingrid's day off—found the number for her. Fortunately some catastrophe in the Frost household—signalled by a loud crash and a screaming child—prevented Madeleine from asking why Alana wanted it.

She dialled the new number and was relieved when Rory

answered, though she heard herself listening for any short-
age of breath that might suggest she'd interrupted what
Jason called a 'snogathon'.

'I'm sorry, I can't make it Friday. I totally forgot I had
another...' Help! She couldn't say date because it wasn't
and he'd made it plain his invitation wasn't either!
'Engagement.'

'Oh!'

He managed to endow the single syllable with so much
downright disbelief that Alana cringed, then, remembering
it was the plain, unvarnished truth, she added, 'Well, I
have! Goodbye.'

She didn't quite slam down the phone, but it might have
sounded like she had from the other end, and she didn't
give a damn.

Wretched man! How dared he disbelieve her?

Bad temper propelled her out of the bedroom and carried
her on swift strides through the living room to the kitchen,
where the sight of Jason, gently stroking the injured rabbit
and talking softly to the frightened pet, doused the heat.

'That's wonderful that he's letting you touch him,' Alana
said. 'He'd been so badly mistreated I didn't think he'd
ever trust a human being again.'

Jason smiled at her.

'If I pick him up, would it hurt him?'

'I don't know,' Alana answered honestly. 'But I have to
take him back to the vet on Thursday afternoon. You could
come with me if you like and we'll ask him. When he was
first found, one of his legs was so badly dislocated the vet
considered destroying him, but the X-ray will show if it's
healed.'

'I'd like to come,' Jason said with such unusual diffi-
dence that Alana wondered if Rory had lectured him on not
making a nuisance of himself. But surely that would have
made him more belligerent.

With Jason's help—he insisted he was an experienced

barbeque attendant—Alana prepared their meal. Jason, she discovered, ate anything and everything—'Mum said it was bad manners to be fussy'—and as they ate he pronounced himself in favour of Alana's potato salad—'I love the crunchy bits of bacon in it, Mum didn't do that'—and the special, not too hot chilli jam she suggested would be just as good as tomato sauce—which she didn't have—on his steak.

She served the meal on the small table on the balcony and they ate looking out over the now quiet street and the neighbouring houses.

'Great!' he said, pushing away his plate and sitting back in his chair. 'But you should get some tomato sauce—you can't have sausages without it.'

They argued amiably about the merits of tomato sauce, moved on to other condiments, then Jason's Siamese cat leapt down onto Alana's balcony, startling them. Apparently finding who she was looking for, she took another delicate leap onto Jason's lap.

He stroked the cat and held it to his face.

'Mum loved this cat. She died, you know. One day she was picking me up from school and she had this headache, and by the next week she was in hospital with a brain tumour. She had an operation, then a lot of chemotherapy that made her very sick and then she died anyway. Rory came and stayed with us. She was his sister and they didn't have either of their parents. Both of them died before I was born, so my only grandparents are my father's parents and I don't see much of them.'

The cat purred and nuzzled its nose against his head, as if intent on offering sympathy.

'I didn't know my father or his parents.' Alana spoke quietly, offering a little of her own story in return. 'Apparently, when my mother found she was pregnant he didn't want to know about it. So my mother brought me up, with help from her family, but then she died when I was young, too, though not as young as you. I was eighteen,' Alana told him. 'You don't ever forget and you don't ever stop missing the person who dies, but it does get easier after a while. Especially if you keep busy enough to not think about it too often.'

Jason nodded. 'Rory says that's why going back to school will be good for me, but I won't know anyone there, and everyone will have their own friends and won't want a dork like me.'

He looked so desperately unhappy that Alana felt her heart squeeze tight with shared emotion.

'It takes a bit of time to find friends that suit you, but if the school has a tennis team, they'll be so keen to have you on it you'll be fighting off people who want to be friends with you. What school are you considering?'

'There's a state high school just up the road, but Rory wants me to go to St Peter's. It's kind of a brother school to the one I went to in Sydney, and the one he went to, and the grandfather I didn't know went to as well.'

Alana chuckled.

'You don't seem too keen on all this tradition.'

'It's not that, it's no girls. It's an all-boys school—isn't that totally uncool?'

She was aware she was sailing uncharted waters—what did she know about adolescents? She remarked that she'd been to an all-girls school mainly because the sports programme had been better. 'I know some of the state schools have good sports teams, but most of them can't offer a full range of choices. I did tennis, rowing and kendo, but other girls played soccer, or netball, or went in for athletics. Before I left they were even offering golf tuition.'

Interest had sparked in Jason's wary eyes. The cat had settled on his knee and he stroked it absent-mindedly.

'Kendo. That's like judo, isn't it?'

'There's a certain connection with the philosophy. Kendo is a different Japanese discipline, and relates more to fencing because it's based on swordplay. Only beginners like me don't get to use swords. We use a long stick called a shinai, which has a piece of string from one end to the other to represent the sword blade.'

'Sounds wicked. Do you still do it? Do you have the gear?'

Which explained why, when she opened the door to Rory for the second time that evening, she was wearing a heavy metal-grilled helmet and hard, padded body armour.

'I guessed you'd change before he came, but is he so threatening?'

The man was smirking!

'Ya, pow!' Jason shrieked, advancing with the shinai.

'At the moment, yes,' Alana said, pulling off her helmet then shrieking herself as strands of hair tangled and stuck in the metal joins.

'Ha. Damsel in distress,' Rory said, stepping forward so he could take the helmet from her hand. 'Stand still, I'm good at this. I considered surgery at one time because a professor said I had such nimble fingers.'

'Female professor?' Alana asked, practically squirming with embarrassment and perhaps just a teensy bit of skittish physical reaction.

Well, maybe more than a teensy bit if the goose-bumps on her arms were any indication… And the way her bones were threatening a melt-down…

Rory's laughter made things worse. The deep rich noise held such genuine delight it once again surprised her. Was it her preconceived idea of him that made the laughter so startling?

Or the physical effect it, too, had on her.

Touch, hearing, scent—she had the lot bombarding her now.

'It's a kendo mask,' Jason was explaining to his uncle. 'Alana learned kendo at school. She went to a private school because they had more choice of sports. Have you still got the book about St Peters? Did it list the sports they offer?'

'Yes, I have the book and, yes, I think it lists the sports they offer.'

'Something else to thank you for, though, of course, you'd refuse to accept thanks,' Rory added more quietly, so only Alana heard. Then, in a louder voice, he said, 'Done.' His hand smoothed her hair, hesitating momentarily against one of the long strands, before he stepped away.

And studied her suspiciously.

'What?' she demanded. 'Have I got mask marks all over my face? Dust and dirt? These things have been packed away for ages.'

Rory realised he was staring, but as he'd settled the last strand of hair he'd had such a strong sense of *déjà vu* his mind had gone searching for an earlier situation where this might have happened.

It *would* have happened if he'd kissed her earlier, because in that mad moment in his mind, as he'd leaned towards her, there'd been an urge to slip his fingers through the golden strands and steer her head—those lips—to his.

But it hadn't happened and, far from providing a basis for his *déjà vu*, what that fragment of time had achieved was a further distance between them if the phone call cancelling dinner was any indication.

But further distance was good…

'No, you look fine, though I like your hair down around your face like that.' Jason answered for him. 'Makes you look less like a Dragon Lady.'

As if pleased by the diversion, Alana moved away, her hands going to her neck where they gathered up the pale gold strands and somehow twisted them into a neat knot behind her head.

'Much better I keep the Dragon Lady in place,' she said teasingly to Jason. 'If I start looking too human you'll take advantage of me.'

'Like this?'

He swung the stick he held towards her and she leapt out of the way, but her movement—towards him, not away—must have put him off balance so the long stick struck wildly, collecting a table lamp and sending it to the ground where the ceramic base shattered and the lightbulb exploded with a very satisfactory bang.

Rory opened him mouth to yell at his nephew, but Alana stepped between them, taking the stick from Jason then saying calmly, 'I've always hated that lamp. You know where the dustpan and brush are kept, Jason. Would you get it while I turn off the power?'

The boy was white-faced, stricken no doubt by guilt, and though Alana's words had been intended to ease the situation, Rory could see the tension he knew so well had returned to Jason's shoulders.

He turned to Alana, furious because with Jason he always seemed to be taking one step forward then two steps back, and right now he needed someone to blame.

But as Jason sidled back into the room and, without being asked, knelt to sweep up the shattered china, Alana held up her hand to stop whatever Rory had been about to say.

'I know you're furious with me,' she said—to him, not Jason, 'and I don't blame you. I shouldn't have been mucking around with kendo gear in a small flat. But Jason knows it was my fault, and he's also learned a valuable lesson. If he does take up any sport involving swords or long sticks, practise in a gym or outdoors.'

She knelt beside the boy, and with a casual 'Thanks, Jase' took the tools out of his hand and finished the job.

Rory shook his head.

He *had* been going to blame her but, seeing the two of them working together, he realised if he had, Jason would have stood up for her. By taking the blame herself, she'd defused the situation that could have developed between himself and his nephew.

Who'd also let Alana get away with calling him 'Jase', a nickname which, up to now, only his mother had been allowed to use.

Rory watched the pair, now jostling each other like two children, and though his body had told him more than once that it wouldn't mind the odd jostle with Alana, this closeness between them was unsettling for other reasons, ones he couldn't quite figure out—yet—but which were no less strong for being inexplicable.

Had she felt herself to be the subject of his thoughts that she turned, the pale eyes with their dark fringe of lashes looking almost silver in the artificial light?

'I'm sorry. Did you come down for some reason? Is it time for Jason to go? I should have asked about his curfew times.'

'What's curfew?' Jason asked, standing up and taking the dustpan from Alana. 'I'll empty this.'

'It's when people have to be off the streets in troubled times, or when kids have to be in bed,' Alana explained when he returned from the kitchen.

'Huh!' the lad scoffed. 'I don't have to be in bed at any special time.'

'No?'

Rory was careful to make the word sound as casual as possible. Regular bedtimes had become lost in the confusion of Alison's illness and death, but since they'd shifted up to Westside he'd tried to reinstate them. One of the many things Jason had found to rebel against.

'I'm thirteen now—' Jason began, but Rory, who'd heard the argument 'I can tell when I'm tired' so many times before, held up his hand.

'We'll talk about it later. I came down to get you because Drusilla wants to talk to you about what movie you want to see on Friday. Apparently there's a water fun park not far from here where they show night movies.'

'Night movies in a swimming pool? Cool, man!'

He shot out the door, then hurtled back seconds later.

'Thanks for dinner, Alana!' he said, then disappeared again.

But the uncle remained, and Alana, feeling uncomfortable in his presence, sought the easy way out—Jason as a topic of conversation.

'He's a good kid,' she said. 'Considering what he's been through.'

Rory looked startled.

'He's talked to you about it—about his mother's death?'

Alana shrugged.

'Not much, just mentioned that she had cancer, had an op and chemo, then died anyway.' She hesitated, then realised there were any number of huge gaps in the story.

'He didn't mention a father—I guess as you went down to Sydney when your sister became ill, there wasn't one around at the time. Does he have one with whom he's in contact?'

Rory's blue eyes darkened, and he leaned back against the wall as if suddenly too tired to stand. Alana realised she should have invited him to sit, but she wasn't sure she wanted an imprint of Rory Forrester's body left in one of her lounge chairs.

Especially now…

'Not noticeably so,' Rory was saying. 'Paul McAllister walked out on my sister when Jason was eight months old. He wasn't an easy baby, colicky, hyperactive, never sleeping, and that was excuse enough for Paul. He was a high-flying executive and shouldn't be expected to handle the broken nights. He believed Alison should have hired a nanny and shut both the nanny and Jason in some far part of the house. Alison's insistence on looking after the baby herself was another problem between them.'

'So he walked out. Easy for him!'

'Exactly, but probably the best thing for my sister. She made a good life for herself and was a wonderful mother to Jason. Until I took the job up here I lived in the next street so, apart from a year when I worked in the UK, Jason has always had a male presence in his life.'

Fighting an inner reminder of just how male that male presence was, Alana came to grips with the conversation.

'And the father—Paul? He didn't keep in touch—didn't see Jason as he grew up?'

'Never! Not once! No birthday or Christmas presents, no maintenance, and, of course, Alison was too proud to fight for it.'

Alana frowned at him.

'It happens,' she said, 'but there's something else, isn't there? You sound as if this man isn't totally in the past.'

'Was, but not is!' Rory ground out. 'Now, thirteen years later, he's decided he's Jason's father.'

'He wants the boy back?'

Rory nodded, then he sighed.

'And he'll probably get him,' he said grimly. 'If I can't pull some miracle out of the hat to convince the courts he's better off with me.'

He nodded abruptly at her, as if he felt he'd said too much, and opened the door, turning back, as his nephew had, to say an abrupt, 'Thanks.' Then departing before she could refuse to accept his gratitude.

Alana picked up the lampshade, grimaced at it, then found a rubbish bag and shoved it in, realising, as she tied the yellow tape, that it was probably the last reminder of her relationship with Brian.

She chuckled to herself. During the five years they'd spent together, Brian had dominated every aspect of her life—including choice of furnishings. Desperately in love—or perhaps, after the death of her mother, desperately in need of someone to love—she'd thought only of pleasing him, so she'd praised his choices, been guided by his advice and had never questioned that he would always be right.

Until she'd been walking past the local vet's surgery one

afternoon and heard an argument over a cat. Stubby had come into her life! Agreeing with the vet that a healthy if tailless cat shouldn't be put down, she'd carried the animal home, only to find after five years with the man that Brian hated all animals.

He'd insisted she take it back to the vet's but in an icon-oclastic dropping of scales from her eyes, she'd seen Brian as he really was, a bumptious, domineering egomaniac.

She'd packed her clothes, taken the lamp—because she'd only recently bought it and had paid for it even though it had been his choice—and the cat, and had walked out, stay-ing first with Gabi and Alex, then moving into this flat when it had become vacant.

Five years ago!

Had it really been five years since she'd made that great escape? And what had happened in her life since then?

Plenty at work, but as far as relationships were con-cerned, not a thing. Oh, she'd been out with various men, some lasting one date, others a few months, but nothing more meaningful than a few laughs and the sharing of good times.

She swung the rubbish bag as she made her way down to the big garbage bins outside the basement car park. Did the lamp's destruction signal freedom at last? An escape from the shadows Brian had cast over her life?

Alana didn't really believe she'd been nursing any sub-conscious hangover from the relationship, though Gabi, Kirsten and Daisy had all at times suggested she might be. Kirsten had even gone so far as to point out that only some-one who'd gone into a bad relationship with a man because she'd been physically attracted to him could possibly spout the rubbish Alana did about love growing out of friendship and trust, while Daisy had often remarked that physical attraction was very definitely part of falling in love and she was wrong to deny it a place in the equation.

Ha! Wrong, was she?

She didn't think so.

Anyway, the meeting with Jeremy on Friday night might signal a whole new beginning.

She smiled to herself, but the excitement dimmed a little when she remembered the other offer she'd had for Friday night.

Damn Rory Forrester for intruding into her thoughts! Surely she hadn't got one shadow finally out of her life, only to find another one sneaking in while the door was still open...

CHAPTER SIX

THE week passed swiftly, partly because Jason's advent into Alana's life meant her usual activities, even a visit to the vet with the rabbit, took a little longer than usual. It also helped that she'd decided to keep herself so busy at work she barely had time to notice Rory's regular—and so far extremely punctual—presence in her ward.

Bessie Oliver had been transferred to a respite bed in a nursing home while arrangements for her to move into the new hostel were completed, but an influx of new geriatric patients highlighted the need for more specialised geriatric services, either at Royal Westside, or in some other city hospital.

So when Ted Ryan, who shared her concern for her elderly patients, came in to see a new admission on Friday afternoon, she all but dragged him into the small doctors' office off the ward to talk to him about it.

Only to find Rory already there, using the computer, though he doubtless had a much superior machine—and a secretary—in his office on the fourth floor.

'Alana, Ted.'

He nodded to both of them, but his voice was ultra-cool—cold cool, not Jason's cool—while his face was a frozen mask of displeasure.

'Sorry, I didn't know anyone was in here.' Alana blurted out, coping with the usual physical manifestations of seeing Rory, as well as shock at the forbidding look on his face. Speech seemed the best option. 'I wanted to talk to Ted about this new influx of geriatric patients. There was talk of St Mary's Hospital, on the other side of the river, setting up a special geriatric department, but it apparently hasn't happened, or we wouldn't still be getting so many elderly patients.'

She hesitated then added, 'But we could talk in the tearoom if we're disturbing you.'

Rory waved his hand as if to say it didn't matter, and Ted, obviously not afflicted with goose-bumps, took it as an invitation to stay.

'It is set up,' Ted said, coming further into the room and propping himself against the desk so she could have the second chair. 'But it's like motorways—by the time they're built, they're never wide enough. St Mary's specialist geriatric ward filled up the day it opened and has been full ever since.'

'Why? Are they taking chronic patients as well as acute cases, or using beds for respite until nursing-home placements can be found?'

'They're taking chronic cases, certainly. As we do with people like Mr Briggs, and your friend Bessie Oliver.'

'But they're admitted with an acute condition,' Alana reminded him. 'Something that needs to be treated immediately so their general health is stabilised.'

'I imagine the same thing's happening at St Mary's.'

'So, might not a city this size need a special geriatric ward here as well as at St Mary's?' Rory asked.

Alana flashed a smile at him.

'Of course it does, but try to convince the State Minister for Health of it. Senior physicians have been trying to get funding for years. The latest argument is that it's discriminatory—age discrimination—and very definitely not the thing to do.'

'Then how did the other hospital—St Mary's—get funding?

'Some of it's private,' Ted explained. 'The rest was part of an arrangement with a previous government and it's tied into hospice funding as well. St Mary's runs a hospice, not on site at the hospital but in a suburban area nearby.'

Rory nodded.

'It's not my field, but I've plenty of older patients and I can see the discrimination point. Not so much as a discrimination issue but from the social side of things, surely someone like Mrs Armstrong would be happier in a ward with younger people around her than in a ward totally made up of her peers, some of whom would undoubtedly be senile?'

Alana, who'd come far enough into the small room to lean on the back of the chair, nodded her agreement.

'Yes, but what's the answer? You did a round earlier. With this sudden spell of hot weather we've had nine admissions in three days of elderly people who've become dehydrated, either because they're simply not drinking enough water or because they've eaten food which has probably gone off and given themselves acute diarrhoea. In one case, an elderly woman who lived alone fell, and lay on the floor for thirty-six hours before a neighbour who hadn't seen her around called the police. That was Mrs Reid—the potassium levels in her blood were high enough to have killed her by the time she was brought in. With Mr Hepchik, it's caused renal failure as well, and Mrs McConachie was admitted with such severe arrhythmia she wasn't expected to live through the night.'

'So you're virtually a geriatric ward anyway? Is that what you're saying?'

Alana shrugged.

'Not really, but, yes, we are heavily weighted with older patients, and they stay longer than younger ones because it's easier to stabilise them in Eight B than shift them around to other parts of the hospital. What bothers me is that so many of their admissions are preventable. If the hospital had specialised geriatric services, we could help integrate the community services already available—home help, community nursing, meals-on-wheels—so older people living on their own would have a kind of umbrella of care over them at all times.'

'I like that idea,' Ted said, beaming his usual cheerful and approving smile in Alana's direction. 'And the phrase—"umbrella of care"—do you mind if I borrow it for a paper I'm writing?'

Alana nodded her agreement, but her attention was focussed on Rory, who seemed far less enamoured of the notion. In fact, from the scowl on his face, she'd have to guess he hated it.

She was about to ask what objections he had to it when Ted was summoned to Eight C. Deciding a tête-à-tête with Rory Forrester wasn't what she needed, Alana was preparing to follow when his voice, as much as what he said, stopped her stone dead.

'Is he the "other engagement" you have tonight? Was that why you were seeking the privacy of this room? For a preliminary skirmish? Or to make final arrangements?'

Rory was aware that the answers to these questions were none of his business, and from the look on Alana's face, she was about to tell him just that. But they'd come roaring out of some inner murk in his mind—presumably the place where he'd been shoving all the things he didn't want to think about right now.

Or ever, really, though doubtless he'd have to some time.

He eyed the woman who stood just inside the door, staring at him with a mixture of anger and disbelief so strong it was obvious she was having trouble finding the words with which to berate him.

Then her eyes narrowed, and her cheeks grew pink, and the words she'd needed came slicing through the air.

'Ted Ryan is a friend of mine, and has been for many years, and while I don't give a flying fig what you think of me, I'll be damned if I'll let you smear his good name with some irrational fancy about him being interested in me as anything other than a friend and colleague.'

She spun away, opened the door and strode out, then

whipped back around. 'And I'm not so desperate for a man I'd *ever* have a relationship with someone else's husband.'

The door shut—firmly—behind her, and Rory held his head—he still hadn't had that haircut—in his hands and groaned.

Hell, she was beautiful when she was angry!

And just seeing her had his body behaving in ways it hadn't behaved for years, while his mind was obviously developing signs of collapse that it had thrown up those stupid suspicions he'd harboured once before about Ted and Alana.

Though she *had*, with her hand around his wrist, dragged Ted into the room just now. What was a man supposed to think?

As little as possible about Alana Wright was the answer to that question. Right now, Jason was his first priority. He had to help the boy settle into his new life, find his feet at a new school and develop friendships with his peers. In the months preceding Alison's death, Jason had cut himself off from his friends—perhaps, Daisy Rutherford had suggested, because he hadn't been able to handle their sympathy towards him—but Rory didn't need Daisy to tell him boys had enough problems getting through adolescence without the added burden of being a loner or misfit.

This concern had prompted Rory to offer to find a job in Sydney so Jason could remain in his old school, but the boy had said he'd rather get away—start somewhere new. Rory could kind of understand this, as he felt a little of it himself.

His pager vibrated against his chest and he remembered he was supposed to be at a specialists' meeting. Good thing he wasn't taking the tetchy Miss Wright to dinner—his experience of such meetings suggested he might be very late leaving the hospital.

So late in fact, Rory didn't get back to Near West until nearly nine when, rather than face fixing himself a meal in an empty flat, he turned into Mickey's Bar and Bistro, pushing open the door and waiting for his eyes to adjust from the light in the well-illuminated foyer to the dimness of the bar.

He saw the hair first, gleaming like a beacon in the shadows—a cascade of blonde hair frothing around the shoulders of a woman who sat at the far end of the bar, her back to the door, her attention totally focussed on the over-developed and trendily dressed male sitting beside her. Not that it could possibly be the woman from the concert. After all, there must be thousands of blondes in Westside. Possibly tens of thousands.

But his body believed it had recognised her, and as he walked towards the bar he wondered if maybe it was an age-related reaction. Once you turned thirty-five, blondes became super-attractive! Didn't rich old men inevitably choose a blonde as a trophy wife?

The middle-aged man—Mickey—behind the bar approached him, and as Rory introduced himself, the blonde, perhaps hearing his voice, turned.

Alana Wright! It *had* to be! When fate decided to knock you down, it usually crunched you underfoot.

So she'd turned him down for a date with a too-good-looking-to-be-true body-builder. He had to be one. No one else had shoulders like that. Or maybe he was wearing shoulder pads, like American footballers.

All this flashed through his mind while Mickey—he'd introduced himself by now—waited patiently for his order.

'I really need a meal—am I sitting in the wrong place?'

He could hear voices and the noise of cutlery coming from the far side of the horseshoe-shaped bar.

'You can order here, and I'll find you somewhere to sit when the meal's ready,' Mickey said, slapping a menu on the bar. 'Do you want a drink while you decide?'

Settling on a half-Scotch and soda, Rory picked up the

menu, but his mind was more on the blonde at the other end of the bar.

She'd nodded acknowledgement of his presence, then turned back to her friend.

Was he just a friend?

Or had Gabi Graham been wrong, and Alana was seeing this man seriously?

It's none of your business, he told himself, but the protest was unbelievably weak. He couldn't see Alana without being aware that he very much wanted to make her his business, one way or another.

Just not right now!

He glanced through the menu and ordered a veal dish with prawns and avocado—going for something fancy as he and Jason existed on steak, potato, carrots and peas, or pizza. Though now Drusilla had installed herself in the kitchen, there was more variety, and for when she left, thanks to Gabi, he had the phone number of a Chinese restaurant which delivered to the building.

'Hi, there.' Gabi appeared, right on cue. 'Alex and I are eating over the other side of the bar—mainly to protect Alana from an axe murderer. Won't you join us?'

'Axe murderer?' Rory repeated, wondering if maybe living in this building did something to people's brains.

Gabi laughed.

'Not really—Jeremy's probably just the harmless accountant he claims he is, but Alana chose Mickey's for a first meeting with him because she felt safe here, particularly with friends around for back-up.'

Not a lot of this explanation made sense, so Rory started with the most unbelievable bit of it.

'That fellow with Alana is an accountant?'

'Well, so he said,' Gabi murmured, turning towards the couple as if to study the stud more closely. 'He's certainly not everyone's idea of a number-cruncher, is he?'

'No!' Rory muttered, then remembered the other thing that hadn't made sense.

'You said this was their first meeting—is it a blind date, or what?'

Gabi laughed, then put her hand on his arm.

'Come and sit with us around the other side. Alana has extra-sensory perception when people are discussing her, and she'd kill me if she thought I was talking about it, but it's been so amazing—her and Jeremy meeting.'

This he had to hear! Rory followed Gabi around the bar and through tables dotted with diners to where Alex sat.

Rory shook his hand, but found himself wishing Alex wasn't there—surely Gabi wouldn't indulge in gossip in front of her husband.

'I was about to tell Rory about how Alana and Jeremy met,' Gabi said brightly, showing Rory how little he knew about women. 'You know the first part, Alex, so you tell it.'

'Rory doesn't want to know,' Alex protested, and Rory, who very much did want to know but didn't know how to say so without sounding as if he did, slumped into a chair and decided it was all too much for him anyway, and the sooner he got Alana out of his mind, the better.

'Well, I'll tell him,' Gabi declared.

She flashed a smile at Rory and he wondered if she'd read his mind—or maybe his body language—because she certainly *knew* he wanted to know.

'When Alex flew back from Scotland towards the end of last year, he sat next to this woman who ran a computer dating service—well, not so much a dating service as a cyber meeting place for singles. Then when Alana was looking for a man for Kirsten, she remembered this and enrolled Kirsten and herself with the service, and suddenly there's Jeremy, talking to her in a chat room. Up to tonight, she'd never met him, though they've been emailing each other for ages.'

Gabi beamed at Rory as if all this conversation made perfect sense, but—who the hell was Kirsten and why did she need a man?

'Isn't it amazing?' she demanded. 'I think it's so exciting. It's almost like the old days of mail-order brides.'

Alex laughed.

'According to Beth, the woman on the plane, it's nothing like the old mail-order brides. Those women didn't have a clue about the man to whom they were travelling. Oh, they might have exchanged a couple of letters, but anyone can make themselves sound good on paper.'

'Even axe murderers?' Rory suggested, and Gabi and Alex both laughed.

'Maybe there *is* a similarity,' Alex conceded, then he went on to ask Rory how he was settling in at Royal Westside, and did he have any first impressions he'd like to share?

Shop-talk took over, and Rory, as he later said goodnight to the couple in the foyer—they were going for a walk before turning in—was surprised to realise how much he'd enjoyed it.

And said as much.

'You've probably not had a lot of adult company lately,' Gabi said to him. 'I imagine helping Jason through the loss of his mother, while coping with your own loss, has taken up most of your free time.' She smiled warmly at him.

'Feel free to join us any time, or if you need someone over the age of thirteen to talk to, give us a call. I'm cutting back to part-time work from the end of next week, and Alex is back on day shift so he'll usually be home for dinner.'

'Thank you,' Rory said, and found he meant it.

But spending a pleasant evening with the Grahams hadn't entirely taken his mind off Alana. He'd tried to see if she was still in the bar as they'd walked out, but the place had been crowded and, without being obvious about it, he hadn't been able to see as far as the back corner.

He glanced that way now, but curtains hid the patrons from people in the foyer, though he could always go in for a nightcap…

Telling himself it was none of his business where Alana was—or how long she stayed out with her muscle-bound accountant-slash-axe murderer, he took the stairs up to the third floor, thinking the exercise would not only do him good but might help him stop thinking about cascading blonde hair falling seductively over a severe black suit.

Once upstairs, he sat down on the sofa bed he'd bought to replace the couch, but although it made up into a more comfortable sleeping arrangement, as a place to sit it was terrible. For a moment he thought longingly of his old recliner, but because he'd been concerned about shifting Jason away from his home and friends, he'd brought furniture from Alison's house rather than his own so Jason would at least have familiar things around him.

Jason! Was he OK? He seemed cheerful enough, thanks mainly to having found a friend in Alana, but Monday would bring another hurdle when he started school. However, since reading that St Peter's did indeed include a variety of martial arts in their sports curriculum, the school issue had become less volatile.

More thanks to Alana…

His groin tightened just thinking about her, but that was probably because of the lengthy period of celibacy—thinking about any attractive woman would cause groin-tightening.

'Hi, we're back!'

Drusilla led the way through the door, and Rory amended his thought. Not quite any, though Drusilla, an extremely attractive brunette, had made it plain she wanted him.

He turned to Jason, asking about the movie and, now he knew him so well, reading the body language behind the words.

'The movie was great!' But the company! A roll of eyes

in Drusilla's direction conveyed this last phrase. 'We went to a restaurant after.'

More eye-rolling—but Rory pretended he didn't see. The lad had to get used to eating out at places other than fast food outlets.

'And I'm taking him shopping tomorrow. His clothes are a disgrace,' Drusilla announced. Eye-rolling gave way to a mutinous tightening of lips, and though Rory privately agreed that too-long jeans trailing down over untied joggers and shorts with the crutch down near the knees looked appallingly untidy, he knew it was a kind of youth uniform and accepted it as such.

'Didn't you have a tennis game lined up tomorrow?' he said, offering Jason a way out.

'Tennis games don't last all day,' Drusilla pointed out, and Jason, who'd grabbed Rory's lifeline with a grateful smile, looked gloomy again.

'No, but we have to discuss a coach for him, and do the final shopping for school.'

Drusilla, realising she wasn't about to get her way, frowned at Rory.

'He's my nephew, too,' she said. 'I'm entitled to spend some time with him.'

Like you have over the past thirteen years? Rory would have liked to have said, but he bit his tongue. Though her brother had defected totally from the family, Drusilla had kept in touch with Alison and had sent Jason cards for his birthday and Christmas. And Alison, especially conscious of family in the way children who'd lost their own can be, had invited Drusilla over quite frequently.

Though Drusilla had only come when it had suited her.

But antagonising Drusilla wasn't in the game plan. If she decided to side with her brother in the battle for custody of Jason, she could be a powerful force.

'And you can,' Rory said. 'After the tennis, we'll all go shopping for the final things for school, then have lunch somewhere. I was reading about a restaurant on the river that had a special weekend smorgasbord.'

Jason did his eye-rolling again, but Rory ignored it. Drusilla was right—she was entitled to spend some time with him.

Placated, their visitor headed for the kitchen, announcing she'd make hot chocolate for all of them.

'None for me,' Rory said quickly, aware of how he'd puffed climbing the stairs and determined to get fitter.

'Or me,' Jason said. 'I'm off to bed. I want to get up early in the morning, swim some lengths to warm up before tennis.' He grinned at Rory. 'No way I'm letting a woman beat me again!'

He called goodnight to Drusilla and headed for his bedroom, and Rory, concerned he'd given Jason the impression there really was a tennis game on, followed him.

'I made up the tennis-game thing,' he said, when they were safely inside the bedroom. 'To get you out of shopping with Drusilla.'

Jason grinned at him.

'I know, but I saw Alana as we came in—boy, is her boyfriend built—and she said to give her a call if I wanted a game over the weekend. I just didn't think fast enough to use it as an excuse.'

Rory, who'd been feeling guilty about the pretence, watched Jason lift the receiver of the phone on his desk.

'You're phoning Alana now?'

Jason shrugged.

'Sure. She was going up to her flat at the same time we came in, so she and Muscles wouldn't have had time to be doing anything yet.'

Rory flinched at the 'doing anything' phrase and wondered just how much Jason knew of the facts of life. Most things, probably.

Jason was talking to her now and smiling, so she'd obviously agreed to a game, but it took all Rory's self-control not to snatch the phone out of his nephew's hand to demand to know why she'd invited a stranger back to her flat.

Alana put down the phone and turned back to where Jeremy had lifted a corner of the blanket over the bird cage and was viewing her bald parrot with something approaching horror.

'It's got no feathers,' he said, and she grinned at him.

'No. Terrible, isn't it?'

'But why do you keep it?' he asked, and she knew this relationship wasn't going to go any further. Jeremy was a gorgeous-looking man, and she'd known from their email correspondence that they shared many interests, but nothing had sparked between them.

Now she made the coffee she'd offered, while explaining how she'd come to adopt Rosie the parrot. But her mind was on relationships and she was, reluctantly, admitting to herself that though, for some people, her theory of love growing slowly out of friendship and mutual respect might work, it certainly wasn't going to happen between herself and Jeremy.

She'd realised that when they'd been sitting in the bar downstairs and Rory had walked in. A tingle down her spine had prepared her, even before she'd glanced around, but it had been the stab of pain in her chest when he'd moved into the light near the bar and she'd seen how tired he'd looked that had been the real give-away.

She and Jeremy chatted over coffee, and in the end it was he who said, 'Well, how do you think it went? Are you interested in meeting again?'

She shook her head.

'You're a really nice man but, no, I don't think so.'

He accepted her decision with a smile.

'You've no idea how many women have said that to me, yet there's a typist in my office who's madly in love with

me—or so she keeps telling me—so I can't be totally un-
attractive to women.'

'So what's wrong with the typist? Doesn't she attract you
at all?'

To her surprise, the manly Jeremy blushed a deep scarlet.

'Well, she does,' he said, 'but she's so blatant about it
I'm worried what people might think. I mean, the whole
office knows how she feels.'

Alana considered this, imagining the situation, going hot
herself at the thought of everyone on her ward talking about
some infatuation she might have. Not that there was one.

'I can see it might have some of your office staff cracking up and making jokes, but surely, if you find you both
like each other, you'll survive that—and it'll soon become
stale news for them.'

Jeremy stared at her in much the same way that patients
who'd come in for tests for cancer looked when told they
were all clear. Hope, joy and disbelief all muddled up
together.

'Do you think—?'

'I do,' Alana said firmly, removing his empty coffee-cup
from his hand so he'd get the message it was time to go.

'But if she goes out with me and gets to know me, she
might find she doesn't like me after all,' he protested, and
Alana sighed.

'That's the risk you have to take, but I don't think that
will happen. You're a very likable man.'

Jeremy beamed at her and stood up, towering above her.

'Thanks, Alana. I will ask her out, and I'll let you know
how it goes.'

She showed him to the door, said goodnight and, after
checking all the animals, headed for the bathroom. A quick
shower then bed.

She hadn't got as far as the shower when a knock
sounded on the door. She grabbed her bathrobe, pleased,

this time she was dry. Peered through the peep-hole and saw Jeremy standing there.

'May I use your phone?' he asked, when she let him in. 'Someone's smashed the windscreen of my car and pinched my mobile. I left it in there because I think it's rude to have phones ringing when I'm out on a date.' He sighed deeply. 'Then, just for good measure, they punctured two tyres.'

She let him in and showed him where the phone was, waiting while he phoned the automobile association and explained his predicament.

A long silence followed, presumably while an equally lengthy explanation was being offered.

'There's been a spate of minor accidents and all trucks are out. It could be a couple of hours before anyone gets here. I'll wait outside.'

'Don't be silly. Wait in here. You'll see the truck pull up outside when it comes—they have flashing yellow lights that will flicker in the windows. Is it too late for another coffee? Or would you like tea this time?'

Jeremy refused both, but accepted the offer to wait in a comfortable armchair rather than on the street.

'You go to bed,' he suggested. 'There's no reason I should be keeping you up as well.'

'It's no bother. Tomorrow's a day off so I can sleep in. Tell me more about your typist.'

Jeremy smiled.

'*My* typist?' he teased, but he did begin to talk, describing the young woman, Marcy, in such glowing terms it was obvious he was attracted to her.

'Why *haven't* you asked her out?' she finally demanded.

'Well…' Jeremy hesitated. 'She's kind of scatty. Not in her work—it's excellent—but her looks and her behaviour—young, you know. And I like that, but she's not what you'd have in mind as an accountant's girlfriend.' He paused again. 'She wears very short skirts.'

'And her legs are hideous?'

Jeremy blushed again.

'No, no, she's got great legs.'

'Well?'

Alana knew exactly what he was saying—or not saying. It was shades of Josh Phillips's reservations about Kirsten, who was the trendiest dresser at the hospital. But part of love was accepting people the way they were, not expecting them to change, and Josh had finally realised that.

Perhaps Jeremy would, too.

She asked more questions, gathering more information than she'd ever needed to know about Marcy while, she hoped, Jeremy came to the realisation that he cared for the woman more than he'd let himself believe.

True to the warning, it was more than three hours before the flashing lights beyond her window told them the rescuers had arrived.

'I won't come down. You'll be OK?'

Jeremy assured her he could manage now and when she opened the door to see him out he dropped a light kiss on her cheek.

'Thanks,' he said, and his smile told her he meant it.

I could almost take over Daisy's job, Alana thought as she waited for the lift to arrive so she could wave goodbye.

The lift pinged to announce its arrival, and the doors slid open, but even before Jeremy stepped inside, Alana saw the passenger already in it. A man coming down from the floor above. And as a senior physician at the hospital, he'd undoubtedly been called in to an emergency.

From the scowl on his face, he wasn't happy about it.

She waved again, including him in the gesture, but as the lift doors slid closed, she could have sworn his scowl had grown grimmer.

So much for cheery waves!

CHAPTER SEVEN

AWARE that the situation was urgent, Rory drove to the hospital. He set his mind firmly on the problem ahead of him, refusing to consider what the big blond man had been doing at Alana's flat all this time.

Though his subconscious refused the ban on conjectures and kept right on working.

Not that it was hard to guess, the way she'd been dressed.

Not that it was any of his business.

Hypovolaemic shock! That's what he had to think about.

It was a sign of poor tissue perfusion—not enough fluids in the tissues, including brain tissue. The patient presented with low blood pressure, clammy skin, feeble pulse, accelerated heartbeats and rapid breathing. Usually it went along with massive blood loss, but there was no evidence of that in the patient, while scans showed no internal bleeding.

At the level the resident had mentioned, it was lethal, and while staff were already pumping fluids into the man, if they didn't find a cause for his sudden collapse, they wouldn't know what to add to the fluids to rebalance the patient's system.

His blood test showed hypoglycaemia, a low level of glucose in the blood, and this was being addressed by the addition of five per cent dextrose in the saline. According to his wife, he'd been tested recently for diabetes, after complaining of tiredness to his GP.

'I'm glad you're here. He's stabilised slightly but there's obviously something very wrong.'

Doug Weaver was the junior resident on duty and, though Rory had only met him briefly, he'd heard good reports of the younger man.

'Let's take a look,' he said, and saw Doug relax. He remembered the feeling from his early days in hospitals, where calling in a specialist could result in appreciation or a tirade of abuse for not being able to handle things himself.

The patient, Albert Cross, still looked extremely ill, but as Rory examined him, small red marks like tiny burst blood vessels on the man's skin suggested a possible cause.

'See these,' he said to Doug, pointing to them.

'Petechial haemorrhages. I associate them with drowning or suffocation—hanging and the like.'

'They can also occur as the result of fever and for a variety of other reasons, but look at his hands.'

The skin, particularly in the knuckle wrinkles, seemed dark for a man who was ginger-haired.

'Some kind of adrenal insufficiency?' Doug guessed. 'Addison's disease?'

'Not necessarily Addison's disease, but you're right about adrenal insufficiency. We'll ask the lab to check levels of cortisol in his blood and if it's low we'll add cortisol, hydrocortisone phosphate, to the drip, six-hourly doses until the acute symptoms subside.'

Doug turned to the nurse to explain what they wanted, while Rory flipped through the patient's chart, seeking the results of the preliminary blood tests. They were good as far as they went, but failed to show the more complex values of either an increase or decrease in ACTH, the adrenocorticotrophic hormone produced by the pituitary gland to stimulate the adrenal gland into producing corticosteroids.

He ordered further blood tests, asking specifically for what he needed, which should tell him if the problem started in the pituitary gland—with it not producing enough ACTH to start the process in the adrenal gland—or in the adrenal gland, with some glitch in the production of cortisol.

He checked the monitor screen, which showed the heartbeat had stabilised and the oxygen saturation in the patient's blood had improved. Looked at the patient, who was somnolent now rather than comatose.

'Keep him here with a nurse, if there's one available, to monitor him, until you're satisfied he's stable, then admit him, but with half-hourly obs and total bed rest. You know to watch for excessive saline in his blood as a result of the infusion, make sure his airway's kept clear and give him oxygen if he seems to be having any respiratory distress. I'll call in and see him in the morning, and we'll start further investigations on Monday if he's well enough. The point is to stabilise him now and to keep him calm.'

Doug laughed.

'Maybe you'd better see his wife. She's outside and she's the one you're going to have to keep calm.'

Rory glanced at his watch. Facing an anxious spouse wasn't his favourite occupation at four in the morning, but as Albert Cross was likely to be his patient for some years to come, he'd better introduce himself now.

'But why?' Mrs Cross demanded, when he'd explained as best he could and, mindful of Alana's derogatory remarks about 'specialist speak', tried to do it in layman's terms. 'And why now?'

'Why now? It could be he had an underlying problem which was suddenly exacerbated by tiredness or stress.'

'Tiredness or stress—we've got plenty of both,' Mrs Cross told him, her voice rising with a modicum of hysteria. 'My son's girlfriend has just announced she's pregnant, and she's got so many bits of metal studding her body the baby'll come out with holes in it. And my daughter finally decided she wasn't putting up with her husband fooling around so she belted him—hit him with a frying-pan—and walked out, bringing her three kids, all under four, home to Mum and Dad. Now she's probably going to gaol and we'll be stuck with the kids. And you talk about stress!'

Rory shook his head with disbelief.

'I can't imagine how you cope.' He didn't add that he

wasn't sure how Mr Cross would survive with such stress, once released.

'But in the meantime, we'll find out what caused the sudden collapse, and once we do, we'll know how to treat your husband. What to give him to stop it happening again.' Along with the advice given to all adrenal patients to avoid stress as much as possible! Rory had never fully realised just how futile that advice could be.

He thought again of Alana, with her fingers crossed behind her back, but, like her, he knew when reassurance was more useful than blunt facts.

'Look, we're going to keep Mr Cross here. Would you like to see him, just so you know he's being looked after? Then you should go home and get some sleep. It's hard having someone close to you in hospital, so you'll need to look after yourself as well.'

Mrs Cross seemed to crumple, as if what he'd said had brought home the realisation that her husband wouldn't be leaving with her. Or perhaps it was because she'd have to face, alone now for a while, the chaos in her family's life.

'All right,' she said, 'but I don't need to see him. I'm very tired and I think seeing him might make me cry. If you promise me you'll take good care of him, I'll just go home and come back in the morning.'

'I promise,' Rory said, and was pleased when Mrs Cross seemed to relax.

'How are you getting home?' he asked, aware that hospital environs often had unsavoury characters hanging around.

'I've got the car. The ambulancemen who came to the house said to bring the car. They knew he wouldn't be coming home with me, didn't they?'

'I suppose they did,' Rory agreed, then he walked her out to the main door and was relieved to see she'd parked— illegally but at four in the morning it didn't matter—almost right outside the door.

When she'd driven away he went back inside, where a nurse was standing by Mr Cross's bed.

'It's quiet enough for me to stay here,' she said to Rory. 'But he's ever so much better than when he came in, isn't he? I said to Dr Weaver at the time, I didn't think he'd make it.'

Mr Cross did indeed look a lot better than even when Rory had first seen him. Which was good, considering his promise to Mrs Cross.

He drove home, the streets still dark, though he could see the sky lightening in the east. But arriving at Near West gave him no joy whatsoever. After Jason had retired, doubtless to play computer games rather than go straight to bed, Drusilla had insisted she and Rory have a talk.

And though it wasn't easy to hear capital letters in spoken words, he knew she'd imbued the word 'talk' with capitals.

'It's about Paul,' she'd begun, and Rory's heart sank. He knew from friends in the finance industry that Paul's business was in trouble, and guessed that was why Jason's father was suddenly showing interest in the son he'd abandoned. Jason had a very healthy inheritance tucked away and, though it was reasonably secure, Paul was a shifty wheeler-dealer and could doubtless get access to at least some of it should he gain control of Jason's life.

'You know he wants Jason. He's already made an application for custody to the court.'

'I've been notified,' Rory had responded, wondering just where this 'talk' would lead. There'd never been any love lost between Drusilla and Paul.

'Well, my lawyer said you'd have a better chance of keeping Jason if you were married. With your working hours, and having to be on call, Paul's lawyers will argue it's hardly a stable environment for the boy. But if you had a wife…'

Oh, please, tell me she's not going to propose, Rory

pleaded silently, hoping some understanding—and prefer-ably powerful—entity might be listening.

Perhaps mistaking his silence for interest, Drusilla had continued.

'Now, if you'd still been with Rosemary, I wouldn't have suggested this, but according to Jason you haven't seen her for ages. He says you haven't gone out with her since Alison got sick. Not that she'd have been much good as far as being a mother to Jason was concerned. Most lawyers work longer hours than you do.'

Rory had been aware of the need to say something—anything—but his mind had closed up for the night. Possibly for ever, given the blankness between his ears.

'It could just be a marriage in name only—you know, like the marriages of convenience in the old days. Unless, of course, you wanted more. I've always found you most attractive, and at times thought you might be interested in me.'

Thinking of the situation now, as he rode up in the lift, he just hoped none of the horror he'd felt had been reflected on his face. Drusilla was certainly an attractive woman, but she didn't attract *him*.

The lift spilled him out on the third floor and he unlocked the door, though the knowledge that he hadn't been firm with Drusilla about this marriage thing lurked like a nau-seous lump in his gut.

He'd said no—well, he was pretty sure he'd said no, but perhaps not in so many words, definitely not that bluntly, trying not to hurt her as he knew Jason should have contact with his father's family.

He tried to recall that part of the conversation, but though every word Drusilla had spoken remained crystal clear in his head, he couldn't remember quite how he'd phrased his refusal.

If he'd…

No, he was sure he had…

But though he knew he needed more sleep, when he crashed back onto the sofa bed, it eluded him until the sun was well and truly up, and Jason was tiptoeing past him to the kitchen.

Rory pretended he was asleep, and eventually pretence must have turned to reality for he next woke to the smell of coffee and something sweetly delicious being cooked in his kitchen.

'Muffins!' Drusilla said gaily, when he opened his eyes and peered blearily towards his kitchen. 'I bought some blueberries yesterday. Jason said they were your favourite.'

The dazzling smile she was directing his way suggested his 'no' *hadn't* been firm enough. Or perhaps it had been non-existent.

Panic gripped his chest with the ferocity of a heart seizure.

Which reminded him…

He looked at his watch—ten after ten. He should have been back at the hospital before now.

Reached for the phone and pressed the recorded number.

When he asked about Mr Cross, he was put through to Eight B.

'Yes, he's here. Apparently he was supposed to go to Eight C, but there were no beds. We put him into a single-bed room and he's resting comfortably. Do you want blood values from the most recent test?'

'No, I'll come up within an hour and see him myself,' Rory said, and, because he happened to be looking towards the kitchen, saw the disappointment that etched itself on Drusilla's face.

'He's a patient I was called out to in the night,' he said, trying to make it up to her. 'But I've time to eat first. I'll just use the bathroom and be right out.'

From the bathroom, he could hear the sound of tennis balls being hit on the court below, and remembered Jason's match. He tried to squint out through the small bathroom window, but could only see the top of the netting.

Reminding himself that sorting Drusilla out was his first priority, he slipped into his bedroom for clean clothes, then headed for the kitchen.

'You *are* coming shopping with us later?' Drusilla asked, anxiety making her brown eyes look darker.

'Of course,' Rory assured her. 'Left to his own devices, Jason's choice of footwear could give my credit card a heart attack. He also has some strange ideas of what's essential equipment for a thirteen-year-old. Last time we went shopping, I had to drag him away from a pair of boom boxes he wanted to connect to his CD so his already loud music could be enjoyed by the entire building, and probably half the neighbourhood as well.'

He could hear the tennis game from here, too, and though he knew he could see the court from the kitchen window, he wasn't sure he wanted to look out. Women tended to have extra-sensory perception where other women were concerned, and Drusilla might imagine he was looking at Alana rather than at Jason.

A mental sigh sifted through his brain, then his lips tightened when he remembered his last sighting of the blonde from the floor below. Even if he had wanted to ask Alana out socially, that now seemed to have been stymied by the arrival on the scene of the body builder.

He'd missed out by one night.

Missed out on what, you idiot?

In a change from sighing, his brain was now arguing with itself, so it took him a moment to realise Drusilla was speaking.

'So when Madeleine said one of the one-bedroom units in the building would be available next month, I told her to put my name down for it. I have to give references, of course, and I suppose I'll have to get a job just to pay for it while I'm there, but I can usually get temporary work quite easily.'

Madeleine? Madeleine Frost, top floor, kind of building manager for her father who owned Near West.

His brain stopped arguing with itself long enough to offer this information, which was useful in its own way but did nothing to stem the horror of his suppositions.

Was Drusilla saying she was staying on in Westside—that she was staying on in this very building?

Why?

As an aunt-type gesture towards Jason? Or because Rory had given her reason to hope her proposal—proposition, whatever—was of interest to him?

Damn all women to hell!

He broke his muffin and shoved enough of it into his mouth to make speech—well, polite speech—impossible.

He chewed, swallowed, sipped coffee and ate more muffin, hopefully giving the impression of a man in such a hurry he had no time to talk. Not a man in such a panic he had no idea what to say!

'I won't be long at the hospital,' he managed, then amended it. 'Well, I shouldn't be long, but you never know. If I'm not back by two, could you take Jason yourself? He has a list of what he still needs, so don't buy anything that isn't on the list. He has a supplementary card for my credit card and can put his purchases on that.'

'Oh, Rory, is that wise? He's far too young for that responsibility surely.'

Rory finally met her eyes.

'That kid helped me nurse his mother through her final illness. If he's old enough for that kind of responsibility, he sure as hell can use my credit card.'

He stood up, then, realising he'd been close to rude, thanked her for the breakfast and praised the muffins.

'In fact, I'll take another one to eat on the way to the hospital. I'll walk up there so at least I get some exercise

today. I keep promising myself I'll always use the stairs—
great cardiovascular workout, climbing stairs—but more often than not, when I'm coming home, I weaken and take
the lift.'

He was rattling on and knew it, but his level of uncertainty—not to mention anxiety—about Drusilla's motives
in moving to Westside was so high it was a wonder he
wasn't hysterical.

Not a pretty sight, a hysterical middle-aged male, he
thought as he opened the door then bit into his muffin.

He walked down the stairs, because a muffin-eating male
strolling the streets wasn't that good a sight either. Though
tempted to slink around the back of the building to check
on the progress of the tennis game, he directed his feet to
head for the hospital instead.

The late night had taken its toll on Alana, and Jason beat
her easily.

She collapsed onto the garden seat in the gazebo beside
the court, lying full length along it and propping her legs
over the back.

'You should be stretching to warm down,' Jason told her,
bending over to stretch his hamstrings.

'I am,' Alana replied. 'See, my legs are stretched up and
my spine is stretched straight. You nearly killed me, you
little wretch.'

She opened one eye and peered at him.

'Are you organised with a coach yet? You should be
getting more practice than an occasional game with me.'

'Rory was going to ask you about that,' Jason replied.
'What I'd really like is to go to one of the tennis schools
in America, where I can do school and tennis at the same
time. If I leave it until after I finish school here, I'll be too
old to really be good.'

'Rubbish!' Alana retorted. 'Plenty of good players
started later.' She saw his face tighten and guessed he'd

seen her as an ally in this argument. 'On top of that, mightn't going away right now be a bit like leaving Rory in the lurch? I know you lost your mother, but he lost his sister, too. If they were close, he's feeling it.'

She glanced sideways in time to see Jason's infinitesimal nod, and hurried on.

'Besides, you're very young to be so far from home. Why don't you set some goals for yourself? If you were to do well in the Australian Junior Championship by the time you're fifteen, then I'm sure Rory would see the sense in sending you to the best possible coaches. And being a bit older, you'd find it easier to settle in over there.'

Jason's face brightened.

'I'll win the Junior by then,' he declared. 'Come on, how about another game?'

Alana groaned.

'No way, kiddo. But I'm happy to play, say, weekends and Wednesdays, and knock up with you when I can on the other days, but only until you've settled in at school and either have a good coach and regular tennis sessions there, or you get a coach outside school and start working with him or her.'

'You could coach me,' Jason suggested, and Alana felt a spurt of excitement at the prospect of such a challenge.

Then she faced reality.

'No, you need the best. I'm only a stopgap measure. Once you know what's on offer at school, we'll talk again. I know a coach who'd take you on, ex-Davis Cup player, but you don't need two people offering you differing advice, so if the school coach is any good, you could stick with him.'

They talked a little longer, and were laughing about some of the antics of famous tennis players of the past when footsteps sounded on the path that led to the court.

'It's the Dracula-clone,' Jason whispered, and Alana,

realising she didn't have time to protest at the remark, contented herself with a reproachful look.

'Are you ready for this shopping expedition?' a voice demanded—and Alana scrambled to remove her legs from the back of the seat and push herself into an upright position.

That definitely hadn't been a woman's voice.

Jason had walked away, obviously to answer his uncle, and Alana sneaked a look that way. Far from being a 'Dracula-clone', Drusilla was, in fact, a very beautiful woman. Dark-haired, fair-skinned, small and beautifully proportioned. At the sight of her by Rory's side, a wave of totally unexpected, and definitely unacceptable, jealousy washed over Alana.

Suspecting she was flushed with embarrassment, and knowing for certain her faded shorts and skimpy singlet top were damp with sweat and probably grubby as well, she somehow managed to acknowledge the introduction to Drusilla McAllister.

But it was the scowl on Rory's face that grabbed her attention. Surely she didn't look *that* bad.

Or was he scowling because Jason was rattling on about her suggestion that he set goals, speaking as if winning the Junior then going to the States in two years' time was a foregone conclusion.

Rory undoubtedly felt she'd crossed the boundary between casual friendship and family business. Hence the scowl?

'I was only throwing up suggestions,' she said lamely, hoping to eradicate the scowl. 'We talked about coaches as well. I thought he should wait and see who coaches at the school.'

The scowl showed no sign of eradication. If anything, it seemed to be growing fiercer.

So she scowled back.

'Don't let me keep you from the shopping. I'll gather up the balls and you can phone me if you want a hit-up, Jase.'

She heard Drusilla catch her breath, and looked towards the woman, who was watching Jason closely. But the boy didn't seem to notice, simply turning to smile at Alana before demanding of his uncle if they could eat before they shopped.

'You can grab one of Drusilla's muffins and eat it while you change. That should keep you going until lunch,' Rory said, as the three of them turned to walk away.

Alana watched them go, the tall man, the smaller woman, and the lanky teenager between them.

Her heart squeezed with sudden pain.

They looked like a family!

CHAPTER EIGHT

'IF YOU'RE not doing anything else, let's lunch.'

Daisy offered the invitation as Alana was unlocking her door. She spun around, surprised by the suggestion.

'What's with you?' she asked. 'Breakfast with Kirsten and me last week, lunch with me this week? Have you finally decided it's time to break out of your self-imposed exile from the world?'

'Is that how you've seen me?' Daisy asked—as a psychologist would, of course.

'Isn't that how you've been?' Alana shot back at her. Two could play the 'answering a question with a question' game.

'Only because of my working hours. I go out in the day-time during the week, but the rest of you are usually working—or if you're on night duty, you're sleeping. It's only been at weekends I've been anti-social—because of working Friday and Saturday nights.'

'Hmmm,' Alana said, hoping she'd injected a good measure of scepticism into her noncommittal noise. 'But, yes, I'd like to lunch. Give me twenty minutes. Do you want to come in and wait? I've got the Saturday papers.'

'No, I'll wash my breakfast dishes. That way, I'll feel swamped with virtue and can reward myself with a dessert.'

Alana laughed. Daisy had a chronic sweet tooth and, though not overweight, was nicely rounded. But in her own eyes, the extra pounds were a problem so, while forever offering advice to parents whose adolescent daughters were paranoid about their weight, she was always battling her own genetic disposition.

They chose a small café not far from the hospital, walking to it so Daisy could feel even less guilty about the dessert.

'Now, without revealing trade secrets, tell me about Jason,' Alana suggested, when they'd ordered and were enjoying a coffee while their meals were prepared. 'He seems an OK kid to me, so why's he seeing you?'

Daisy didn't answer immediately, then she sighed, blowing air out so audibly that Alana worried about her young friend.

'I don't really think there's anything the *matter* with him, but he's had a lot to handle lately,' Daisy said. 'His uncle's worried that he won't talk about his mother—or about her illness. He—Rory, not Jason—is also concerned that he had to bring the boy away from his old environment at such a time, and the effects that might have on Jason.'

'And?' Alana prompted.

'And what? Isn't that enough?'

'Not really. Are you helping him? Does he want to be helped? Won't he talk about things when he's ready?'

Daisy chuckled.

'I know you've become friendly with him, and that's probably the best thing that's happened to him since moving here. But to answer your questions—I don't know if I'm helping him, and he certainly doesn't think he needs help, and, yes, he probably will talk about things when he wants to. So far, all I've done is talk to him about my work, what I do and how I do it. I've told him I'm there if he wants to talk—about anything at all, not just to do with his mother's death. We've a weekly appointment and so far he's come once to be introduced and for me to explain all this, and for him to tell me he didn't need me—and that's it.'

'Yet you said, that day in the canteen, that he was a mixed-up kid who needed help—that's why you had to talk to his uncle.'

'I still think he probably is,' Daisy replied, 'but until he wants help from me, I can't help him. I may never be able to help him and, to be perfectly honest, he could easily work his way through this by himself. I think what worries Rory is that there's going to be a custody battle with Jason's father, and if the court asks for a psychological evaluation of the lad, and the psychologist picks up problems, Rory might lose him.'

'Hell! He loves the kid, and he loved Jason's mother, and he's the one who was there all through her illness. How could the court take Jason away?'

'For any of the reasons I already mentioned—like Rory living here so far from where Jason grew up.'

'Well, next time I talk to him—Jase, I mean—I'll tell him he'd better get his butt into gear for his next appointment with you and make sure he's sorted before any court-appointed psychologist gets hold of him.'

A waitress arrived with their meals—salad foccacia rolls for both of them—and Daisy waited until she'd gone before replying.

'Don't do that, Alana,' she said quietly. 'For a start, I shouldn't have been talking to you about all of this, but I know you have his best interests at heart. But the most important reason not to get involved in that way is because he sees you as a friend. Someone he's found for himself. A person he likes and who, presumably, likes him. He needs you to continue to be his friend, not his spare psychologist.'

Alana frowned at her.

'But we all do our amateur psychology stuff with our friends. Analysing ourselves and each other, discussing our reactions to just about everything under the sun. It's what friends do.'

'It's what women friends do with each other, and there's a two-way exchange. He can't possibly do that for you, so you doing it for him would leave him in a lesser position in the friendship. Think about the roles we play in each other's lives. We're all different people to others—daughter, friend, lover, mother. Talking to him about stuff he'd expect me to discuss with him would have you stepping out of your role as his friend just as decisively as, say, you suddenly taking up with his uncle.'

'Me taking up with his uncle? You mean romantically? As *if*!'

She hoped she sounded outraged, which was how Daisy would expect her to sound.

Not shivery, tingly excited, which was actually how she felt.

'Yes. I realise it's not likely to happen,' Daisy said, with such certainty Alana had to bite back the 'why not?'. 'But it illustrates what I mean. Because he's an adolescent there could well be a bit of boy-girl attraction in his relationship with you, and even if there wasn't, it would still seem to him—if the pair of you did get involved—that his uncle had stolen his friend. And his attitude to you would change—you prefer his uncle to him and you've also pinched the man who's been his sole support for the last few months.'

Alana heard this very logical explanation through a thick black cloud of gloom that seemed to have settled over her side of the table. Not that it didn't make sense, for it did, and she could even pick up on all the unspoken nuances—like more hurt and loss for Jason—in the basic explanation.

Not that she'd ever really expected to have a rip-roaring affair with Rory Forrester—although, considering it that way, the alliteration made it an even more attractive proposition!

But she *had* been attracted—probably still was—and now Daisy's theories had made him a definite no-go area. Rory Forrester was off-limits.

Something of her thoughts must have been visible on her face, for Daisy was looking anxiously at her.

'What's up? Do you feel I've got it wrong? I could have. I don't claim to know everything.'

Daisy sounded so anxious Alana rushed in to reassure her.

'No, you made perfect sense. I was thinking about the boy, losing his mother at that age.'

She glanced guiltily around, fearing that a plane trailing a banner saying LIAR might immediately swoop over the open-air eating area.

'So, let's get off the Forrester saga and do what women do best. Let's analyse each other's lives. What's prompting you to reconsider your career, apart from the stupidity of the people who phone in to your programme?'

They chatted on but, though Alana felt a certain amount of pride in her composure, a large knot of disappointment remained lodged in her intestines, while the black cloud had turned the world a very colourless grey.

Back home, a major spring-cleaning project suggested itself as one way to get through the afternoon—and ignore the grey cloud and knot of disappointment. Alana started on the spare bedroom, so rarely used it didn't need much attention, but she dusted and vacuumed, changed the sheets so any unexpected guest wouldn't cause a flurry of bed-making, then moved on to the bathroom.

Cupboard first, where, with a garbage bag in one hand, she flung away any ancient almost empty bottles and tubes, reducing the contents to spare soap, tissues and necessities like shampoo, skin cleanser, moisturiser and a small bag containing her cosmetics.

'Most efficient,' she praised herself, when, with tiles and bath gleaming and the floor washed, she dragged the bag out to the living room, where months of old magazines joined the exodus.

Depositing the full bag by the door, she dusted the wooden shutters, then shifted all the furniture into the centre of the room, determined to vacuum bits of carpet that only saw the light of day about once a year.

'Ugh! Does dust breed?' she muttered to herself, then, as she pulled the vacuum cleaner around the room, someone knocked on the door.

Prince Charming for sure! Here with the slipper. And me in my oldest shorts and a filthy shirt and sweat and dirt for decoration!

'It's me. Jason! Are you home?'

She debated pretending not to be, then heard his key slide into the lock and shot across the room to open the door. At least, if there was, as Daisy suspected, any undercurrent of attraction in his friendship towards her, seeing her like this should dispel it.

'I'm spring-cleaning,' she said, though the explanation was hardly necessary.

'It's not spring,' the literal-minded male replied.

'I know that, it just needed doing,' Alana told him, not adding that she'd needed something to occupy her mind and physical work had seemed the best bet. 'Did you want something?'

Had she sounded abrupt, that Jason's ears went pink and the usually vocal young man looked tongue-tied?

'Maybe I shouldn't have come,' he muttered. 'Rory said I shouldn't…'

'So, of course, you did!' Alana smiled her encouragement. 'Come on, spit it out, I won't bite you.'

She won a half-smile.

'It's a favour, and though Rory says it's too big a favour to ask of someone we hardly know—but I do know you, don't I? Anyway, I'd eat upstairs and everything, it's just a bed.'

Alana tried to make sense of the words, but failed.

'What's just a bed?'

'Your bed.' His cheeks went pink, while the ear colour escalated to scarlet. 'Not your bed, of course, but your spare bed. You see, Rosemary's just arrived. She's Rory's old girlfriend from for ever, and she's come up to stay and Drusilla is still here and Rory's already sleeping in the living room so I can't sleep there…'

Light dawned, and though Alana's mind was offering hilarious images of Rory Forrester with two females on his hands—and in his not so large flat—her intestines didn't find it amusing and, really, her first priority should be Jason, still standing pinkly on her doorstep.

'You want to stay? Of course you can. I must have been psychic because I started my spring—OK, autumn—clean in the spare bedroom.'

'Thanks Alana,' Jason said. Then, to her intense surprise, he reached across and gave her a quick hug before dashing off to the stairs to go up to his floor.

'Get the vacuuming done,' Alana told herself, and though she obeyed, the cleaning urge had died—killed by the thought of 'Rory's old girlfriend from for ever'.

It shouldn't worry you—he's off-limits, remember.

She pushed the nozzle of the machine fiercely across the carpet, banging it right up against the wall.

He's not for you, no matter how attractive you might find him.

She slammed an armchair back into its usual position, then decided it might look better somewhere else and dragged it across the carpet to the opposite corner.

Another tap on the door. She was close enough, given where she'd shifted the chair, to open it immediately, saying brightly to her expected visitor, 'It didn't take you long to pack.'

'Was I included in the invitation to stay? It'll only take me a minute to whip upstairs and pack, believe me.'

Rory looked and sounded so harassed Alana was tempted to hug him—just a friendly hug—but the situation with Jason put even friendly hugs out of bounds.

'Oh,' she said instead, as the implications of the urge

shook her composure. Then, suddenly conscious of how dreadful she must look, she took refuge in a babble of words. 'I've already rented out the spare bed but you could have the lounger on the balcony, or I've a spare guinea-pig cage in the basement.' She looked him up and down. 'If you wouldn't find it cramped!'

He smiled and her bones melted and she told herself it was stupid to joke with Rory Forrester, but what else was she supposed to do?

'I came to thank you for agreeing to take Jason. It shouldn't be for long—hell, I hope it's not for long. I... It's my fault...'

He shrugged broad shoulders and looked even more despondent, and again the urge to hug him swept fiercely over Alana—so fiercely she had to clutch the vacuum wand very tightly so her hands didn't involuntarily move towards him.

'I should have told Drusilla to stay somewhere else, right from the start, but I didn't and now, with her there, I can hardly tell Rosemary *she* can't stay, so I need Jason's room for her.'

Huh?

'So it isn't obvious to Drusilla that you and this Rosemary are an item?'

The question slid from her lips before she realised it was there, but once it was out she realised there was more.

'Why? Is it a secret? Jason says it's been going on for ever, you and Rosemary. Wouldn't Drusilla have known?'

Rory said nothing, simply staring at her with a perplexed expression on his face—as if she might be speaking Urdu. Then light dawned in Alana's mind.

'Oh, Rosemary just needs a room. With you already camped in the living room, she needs somewhere to put her gear.'

Shaking his head, and totally uninvited, Rory stepped into her flat and slumped into the chair she'd just pushed over to the corner near the door.

'Women!'

The word held such a degree of loathing Alana was glad he was off-limits, though there were bits of her not taking any notice of the ban and jiggling up and down with delight at the sight of him in her lounge chair.

'I'm a woman!' she reminded him, realising she should stand up for the sisterhood. 'And I'm helping you out.'

'You are not helping me out,' he growled, then shook his head and added, in no less of a growl, 'Well, you are with Jason, but every other way you're driving me insane. You'd think when a man has two women camped in his home, one proposing marriage at regular intervals and the other arriving, no doubt ready to spring a similar offer on him at any moment, the last thing he'd be feeling is sexual attraction to yet another one of the species. You'd think it'd be enough to put him off women for life but, no, the old male urge kicks in and every time I see you, even with dust smeared across your face and rat's-tail hair, I want to throw you over my shoulder, cart you off to my cave and have my evil way with you.'

The growl had become more a grumble by the end of this declaration, but even grumbled it was so startling Alana found her lips opening and closing but no sound coming out. Then one bit of it struck home.

'Rat's-tails? Let me tell you, buster, if you'd been pushing this furniture around your hair might not look its best either.'

He looked up, his blue eyes awash with confusion.

'Is that all you have to say? I tell you I'm attracted to you and you want to make an issue of hair?'

I don't want to make an issue of hair, I'm just so damn confused it was the easiest bit to handle, Alana thought, but she wasn't going to share the confusion with Rory. Best to stick to practicalities.

'You can't be attracted to me,' she said bluntly, though

her heart was telling her of course he could—wasn't she attracted to him right back? 'Daisy said so, and that's that.'

She turned away, surreptitiously tucking a couple of rat's-tails of hair behind her ear while dragging the vacuum cleaner back towards the hall closet. She couldn't remember if she'd done all the corners of the room but, if she hadn't, what the hell.

'Daisy said so?' His disbelief was even more forceful than his words. 'What do you mean, Daisy said so?'

After shoving the cleaner away, Alana slammed the door and, reluctant to get too close to him again, stepped cautiously into the bit of hall that opened into the living room.

'She said it would be terrible for Jason because he sees me as a friend and he'd view any relationship between us as all kinds of betrayal—me liking you better than him, you liking me better than him, you stealing his friend, me stealing his uncle. I think there might have been even more horrible complications but it was all so traumatically believable I stopped listening.'

Rory tried hard to make sense of what he was hearing, but his mind had sloped off down another track. Realising Alana wasn't going to come closer so they could have a proper discussion about this lightning-bolt revelation, he rose to his feet and stepped towards her.

'And just why were you and Daisy discussing a relationship between you and me? Why should it even have been mooted, given the time the body-builder guy spent in your flat last night?'

She'd watched his approach with the wariness of a rabbit caught in the headlights of a car, but now he could see her expression change, through startled to seriously wary, then, with pinkness rushing to her cheeks, to furiously angry.

'The amount of time the *who* spent in my flat? And what business of yours, pray tell, are my visitors? Do you get off on imagining wild couplings among the various tenants of the building? Do you time everyone's visitors or just mine?'

Desperate to redeem the situation, Rory stumbled into a disjointed apology, blaming tiredness, confusion, too many visitors himself, and finally admitting it was none of his business.

'But you and Daisy discussing a relationship between us is,' he added, retreating to firmer ground as he remembered where the argument had started.

'Daisy and I weren't discussing a relationship between you and me,' Alana said, her pale eyes looking up into his with a mix of defiance and sadness he found both disconcerting and incomprehensible. Why should anger give way to sadness? Especially as she must be lying.

'We were talking about Jason. Daisy used the "you and me" situation as an example of the kind of circumstance that could upset a kid with a shaky emotional balance.'

'"Shaky emotional balance"? Did she use those words? Is that what she thinks? Goddammit, why doesn't the woman insist she see him regularly if she thinks he's that bad, instead of leaving it up to him to decide if he wants to talk?'

Well, at least that's got him off the subject of the 'you and me' thing, Alana thought, but now she had Daisy in trouble.

Friendship decreed she should at least try to retrieve the situation.

'She didn't say he *had* a shaky emotional balance, just that, given the changes in his life recently, things could be shaky somewhere inside him. She's given him the option to talk to her any time and, in fact, it was only because I suggested maybe I could tell him that talking to her would be good that she got fired up and told me my role in his life was as a friend, not a counsellor.'

'Or a love interest of his uncle?' Rory murmured, though there was no humour in his voice and his lips were grim.

Yet he was so close all she could feel was the attraction she always felt, only now it was exaggerated a thousandfold.

'The love-interest thing was an example. Truly.' Heaven knew how she managed to get the words out when her chest was so tight with tension it was aching. 'I mean, why would we be talking about something going on between you and me when nothing does, or has, or—?'

'Hasn't it?' he said, the words almost inaudible so she had to lean closer to hear them. 'Is what I feel all one-sided?'

He hooked his finger behind the top button of her shirt and pulled her upper body forward, closing the eighteen-inch gap between them.

'Tell me it's one-sided, Alana.'

The words were whispered so close to her lips there was no way she could have answered, even if he hadn't cut off that option with a kiss that burned through all her barriers, seared its way across her senses, then set her skin on fire. Desire, so akin to pain she gasped, ricocheted through her body, while Rory, perhaps encouraged by the gasp, drew her closer, his hands moulding her body against his, fitting the two of them together until it seemed they were one entity.

Voices, seemingly a long way off, finally penetrated her consciousness and, panicking, she pushed herself away.

'J-Jason's back!' she managed to stutter, then she turned and fled towards the bathroom.

Where no amount of cold water splashed across her face cooled the heat still ravaging her body. Though it did provide her with more rat's-tails than she'd had previously.

The murmur of conversation easily penetrated the closed door and, knowing she couldn't stay shut in the bathroom for ever, she wiped her face, pushed the rat's-tails back again, put her hand on the doorknob and prepared herself to bravely sally forth.

Well, as bravely as she could with a squeamish stomach, unreliable legs and her heart banging so loudly in her chest she suspected both her visitors would hear it.

Though maybe Rory had gone.

Wouldn't that be good?

'You're back quickly,' she said as she emerged from the bathroom. She heard the squeak in her voice and decided she'd missed 'bright and welcoming' by about a mile and hit 'slightly demented' instead.

Jason was shuffling into the spare bedroom with a long sports bag in one hand and a guitar in the other.

She hadn't known about the guitar.

But before she could mention it—maybe question his practice times—she realised he was only the leader of a procession of people, all carrying what presumably were more possessions.

Drusilla came first, with a box of tapes, CDs and computer disks, while behind her was another woman—another beautiful brunette, of course—carrying a small computer with a collection of cords trailing behind it like misplaced entrails.

Rosemary?

'Alana, this is an old friend of mine, Rosemary Jenkins. Rosemary, this is our neighbour, Alana Wright.'

Rory, bringing up the rear with yet another box which one of the women must have been carrying earlier, performed the faultless introduction, but what he made of the quizzical look Rosemary sent him when he mentioned 'old friend' or the dirty look Alana delivered, just seeing him returning to her flat, she couldn't tell. The man's face was an unreadable mask.

'I'm actually also his solicitor, and Jason's as well,' Rosemary said, returning to the hall after dumping her load and putting out her hand towards Alana. 'Though as I was telling Rory, I can't act for him in the custody case because it's a different field of law and I'd also be considered too close—conflict of interests and all that, you know.'

She was charming, chattering on in a light, inconsequential voice, telling Alana things she didn't really need to know—and probably shouldn't know, given that solicitors had as strict rules of confidentiality as the medical profession.

Drusilla and Rory both departed, presumably to get Jason's clothes as surely everything else he owned was already here, but Rosemary hovered, checking out the animal cages, talking to the parrot, possibly waiting for an opportunity to say more, because when Alana headed for the kitchen to get a drink of water—which might or might not help the residual heat from the kiss—she continued talking.

'When Alison was ill, I backed away from Rory, not because I didn't love him—Lord, we'd been going out practically all our adult lives—but because he needed all his energy for Alison and Jason. Then, of course, I had to give the law firm in Sydney notice before I could leave, but with the custody hearing coming up—Rory's case is more likely to be successful if he's married or about to be married—I thought I'd better get myself up here.'

Far too much information! Alana thought as she battled to keep up with the verbal flood. And why? What made this woman think any of this could be of the slightest interest to me?

Except it was—especially the bit about the custody case, and Rory standing a better chance of winning it if he was married.

Very carefully, Alana set her water glass down on the kitchen bench, then she said, 'I'd better see if Jason needs anything.' She walked past where Rosemary was still peering at the parrot, through the living room, down the hall and, after a perfunctory tap on the open door, into her spare bedroom.

'Do you really need *all* this gear for a temporary visit?'

she asked Jason, smiling at him at the same time so he didn't feel he wasn't wanted.

He grinned at her and shoved his empty sports bag under the bed.

'Scared I'll stay for ever?' he teased, and she shook her head.

'It's because of school,' he continued. 'I'll have to do my homework so I need my computer, and I can't do homework without music so I needed the CDs, and Rory's already told me he'll personally rip off my ears if I play it too loud and disturb you.'

'And the guitar?' Alana asked, and saw the now familiar tightness come over Jason's face.

She'd said the wrong thing.

'I won't be loud,' he said. 'I just like to strum it sometimes.'

Alana glanced at the instrument, propped carefully in one corner of the room. It wasn't new, or flashy in the way teenagers' guitars often were. Had it been his mother's?

'That's fine with me,' she said, speaking quietly so she didn't seem to be making an issue of it. 'I love the sound of a guitar.'

She backed out the door.

'I want you to make yourself at home. What do you like to drink and snack on when you're studying? I know Rory said you'd eat upstairs but you don't want to be dashing up there when you feel like a snack. And breakfast. If you just have cereal and toast, you might as well have that here as well. What cereal do you like?'

Jason didn't answer, simply looked at her, while the tightness disappeared and a look Alana couldn't analyse took its place.

'You're being very kind to me, although you hardly know me,' he said.

Had the look been suspicion?

Slapping down the thought, she smiled in what she hoped

was a very reassuring manner and, mindful that she was cutting off for ever any hope of a relationship with Rory, she said, 'But we're friends, aren't we? Friends help each other out. And I don't think friendship depends on how long you know a person but more on how you click.'

She grinned at him, then added, '*And* how clean you leave the bathroom! Just remember we'll be sharing, so mop up any mess before you walk out the door.'

These firm words seemed to restore Jason's equilibrium and, confident now their friendship was also balanced again, she walked away to get a notebook, then returned to ask what food he wanted kept in stock.

'Rory will pay,' he told her. 'But I'm not dependent on him. He's my trustee, and can dole out money to pay for what I need.'

He was speaking with his usual candour, but Alana was still surprised when he continued, in the same matter-of-fact way, 'I'm quite rich. That's why my father suddenly wants me to live with him. Rory's rich, too, so at least I know he doesn't want me for my money. His parents— Mum's parents, too—left a lot of money to Mum and Rory. I think that's why Drusilla and Rosemary both want to marry him.'

'But he didn't just get rich when your mother died,' Alana said, because the flaw in the story was too big to ignore. 'So why didn't they want to marry him earlier? I mean, I don't know how old he is, but he's no spring chicken.'

'Who's no spring chicken?'

The man *would* walk in, right on cue. Suspecting, in his current confiding mood, that Jason might actually answer, she threw him a warning glare.

Did it help?

Not a bit of it!

'You,' Jason was saying cheerfully, while Alana could just as cheerfully have wrung his neck. 'I was telling Alana we've both got money—' great, now if ever anything did happen between us, not that it could, but if it did, he'd think I was after him for the money '—and that's why the Drac—sorry, Drusilla—and Rosemary are both after you, and why my father is after me.'

'It must be nice to be so sought after,' Alana murmured, sidling out of the room so Rory could get in to put down the pile of clothes he was carrying.

'Your money is in trust for you until you're twenty-five,' Alana heard Rory say to Jason as she walked away. 'And if I hear any more discussion of it, or people being after other people for money, I'll cut your allowance back so far you'll need a magnifying glass to read your bank balance.'

He sounded stern, but the scuffling noise that followed suggested they were following up the lecture with a little wrestling—male bonding stuff, Alana guessed.

And she still didn't know what cereal to buy or what snacks to get in for her young guest.

Snacks reminded her of the guinea-pig babies, who must now be teenagers in guinea-pig years as they were always hungry. She cut up an apple and was poking slices through the bars of their cage when heavy footsteps told her the wrestling was done—and Rory was approaching.

Or maybe he was just leaving.

She kept her back to the room so he'd know there was no need to socialise, but the man had less awareness of atmosphere than his nephew. And, knowing he'd stopped, common decency decreed she should turn to face him.

'Well?'

He scratched at his head, and she could have sworn she heard a muttered oath, not quite caught in time.

'You're very good to have him. Please, don't let him make a nuisance of himself. Send him up for meals and, though I know you hate the thought of repayment, just as a gesture—to ease my conscience a minute fraction—could you see your way clear to having dinner with us tonight?

I realise you probably have better things to do, and I have to tell you it's likely to be a bit of a circus.'

'With three women at your table?' He looked so uncomfortable Alana couldn't resist teasing him. 'I'd say it would be a full-blown circus performance!'

'There's no way three could be worse than two,' he told her, both voice and lips adding grim constraint to the words. 'So would you come? I do a mean lamb curry. Unless, of course, you've got a date with the chap you were with last night. Or someone else. Another engagement.'

He floundered on, but Alana was wondering what ulterior motive he might have for inviting her and what excuse she might make to herself, should she accept.

'You haven't answered.'

Grim had given way to grumpy.

'I haven't decided.' Alana found herself smiling. 'To be perfectly honest, I can think of better ways of spending Saturday evening than with two women who are fighting over a man. Drilling a hole through my left eye comes to mind. Or having my toes cut off with a bolt-cutter. Or—'

'OK, I get the picture!' Rory said. 'You don't need to rub it in.'

Then he paused, and a very small smile shifted the contours of his face. Shifted something inside her as well. Seeing those lips move brought to mind—far too vividly— the feel of them.

And the effect of their power on various parts of her body...

'But wouldn't you come anyway? Believe me, I'd be very grateful—undying gratitude. It's just until I work out what to do with them both. I mean, Rosemary's come up here, thinking I needed help. I can hardly kick her out into the street...'

I think you'd find she could fend for herself, Alana wanted to say, but didn't.

'While Drusilla *is* Jason's aunt.'

But wants the uncle, not the boy. Once again Alana didn't voice her thoughts.

She wasn't sure she wanted his undying gratitude either, so was still hesitating when Jason bounced out of the spare bedroom.

'I've written a list for you, but you're not to pay for any of it. Rory will pay, won't you, Rory? And did he ask you about coming to dinner? Please, please, please come, Alana. At least if you're there the other two can't keep sniping at Rory about how a single man can't bring up a child. As if I'm a child anyway. And they talk as if I'm not sitting there right with them.'

His smile, so like his uncle's, curled charmingly across his lips.

'I'll think about it,' she grouched, 'but you could just as easily have asked Gabi and Alex if you wanted to dilute your mix of guests. Or Kirsten and Josh. Or Daisy.'

'I did ask Daisy and she's working,' Jason said, and both Rory and Alana turned to look at him.

But neither asked the question, though Alana guessed Rory was just as anxious to ask it as she was.

The 'when did you see Daisy and why' question. Questions, really.

'I just saw her in the lift.' Jason's explanation came without the questions being asked. 'I figured with a couple of women already fighting over the Dungeon Master, one more would make it interesting.'

He shot a cheeky look at his uncle, and ducked out of the way of Rory's cuffing right hand. Then he caught his uncle's arm and held it, and Alana, sensing another wrestling match was about to begin, held up her hands.

'Out!' she said. 'No fooling around in my flat.'

They stopped. And though Rory began to follow Jason out, he turned and winked at Alana.

'Spoilsport!' he whispered, and she knew he was thinking of a very different kind of 'fooling around'.

Finally alone, Alana sank down into an armchair and tried to work out exactly what had been happening these last… She checked her watch. Heavens, had it only been two hours since Jason had come down to ask to stay?

It was five-thirty now, and she'd started on the living room a little after three, which made it just over two hours.

For her life to change?

But it hadn't changed, she reminded herself. Rory Forrester might have kissed her and confessed the attraction she now knew was mutual, but that didn't change her status as Jason's friend, or alter Daisy's perception of how any shift in that status could affect the young lad.

Who'd already suffered a major loss…

So why, when nothing could come of it, did knowing Rory was attracted to her make her feel light-headed, and her body, even thinking about that attraction, sizzle with the slow burn of desire?

Nothing will come of it.

Nothing *can* come of it.

Could they have a secret affair?

Alana sank her head into her hands while she argued with the bit of brain that didn't seem to be listening to all the other parts. To the ones making the 'nothing' statements.

Of course there would be no secret affair.

Actually, the mere thought of a 'secret' affair in the Near West building was enough to make another bit of brain tissue positively crackle with laughter.

But in spite of all these mental remonstrations, a warmth remained, while a devilish delight bubbled up as she considered the opportunity to observe the machinations of the two women vying for Rory's attention. Maybe dining with them would be fun.

And an excuse to see more of him, even if it was a case of look but don't touch…

CHAPTER NINE

RORY pushed open the door into the stairwell, intending to return to the flat and do something about starting the evening meal. The longer a curry cooked the better it tasted, and the time for taste improvement was diminishing rapidly.

But the thought of his uninvited guests made him hesitate, while the after-effects of kissing Alana still throbbed in his body, demanding physical release.

If he jogged around the block a couple of times…

Glanced down at his footwear—canvas loafers. Hardly jogging gear.

Jason had gone back upstairs, which meant Alana was on her own.

He could go back in and kiss her again.

Sure! his mind derided. Like she's just waiting inside the door for you to reappear?

Like she hasn't seen enough of the Forrester/McAllister household for one day?

Though maybe she'd come tonight, and even if he couldn't touch her, she'd still be there.

And just the thought of seeing her in his flat made him wonder if his body had ever stirred when he'd thought about Rosemary.

Back when they'd first been lovers?

He shook his head, unable to believe he couldn't remember.

His indecision, which had kept him pinned on the second-floor landing of the stairs, was interrupted by a clumping noise that suggested either a herd of elephants had been released from the penthouse or Jason was coming down.

'I came to look for you,' Jason said. 'Come on, it's really creepy up there without you. Drusilla wants to chop up the meat for the curry and Rosemary says you hate anyone helping in the kitchen, but Drusilla's got the cleaver, and any minute now we could be having curried Rosemary in with the lamb.'

Rory laughed but, having felt the vice-like tension in the room whenever the two women were sparring, he knew why Jason needed support.

'I never say no to someone else peeling and chopping the onions,' he told Jason. 'Let's get the cleaver back from Drusilla and you can have that job. I'm sure curried finger of Jason will be tastier than skull of Rosemary.'

Jason joined his laughter, and Rory felt a sudden fullness in his heart.

The arrival of the two women had thrown him off track, and no doubt their presence in his house, and the resultant confusion in his mind, had made him seek relief by dwelling on what was probably nothing more than a passing attraction for his neighbour and colleague.

But laughing with Jason had reminded him of what mattered most. His sister's lad—his closest living relative—a boy who'd already suffered too much in his young life.

In another few years, Jason's life would have stabilised, and though he himself might not be a 'spring chicken'— he'd have to speak to Miss Wright about that comment some time—it certainly wasn't going to hurt him to put his personal life on hold while this happened.

They walked into the flat together, where the sight of the two women in his kitchen tempted Rory to turn tail and run.

'We could go to South America,' Jason whispered, picking up on his uncle's thought waves.

'Not far enough,' Rory whispered back, then he slung his arm around Jason's shoulders and propelled him forward.

'OK, women, out of the kitchen. That's the men's do-main. Now, Jason, while I get everything out, why don't you slip upstairs to see if the Grahams are doing anything tonight? If not, they might like to join us. I'll do a vegetable curry as well, so there'll be plenty of food.'

He felt very pleased with himself as he delved into the refrigerator. If Alana did come, an extra two would dilute her presence somewhat, and if she didn't...

He didn't want to think about if she didn't, he decided, pulling the vegetable drawer right out so he could set it on the bench where he could stand upright to select what he needed.

It turned into a party when Jason found Josh and Kirsten at the Grahams' place, and with the open-handedness of youth invited them as well.

'I was sure you hadn't prepared for a full-scale invasion,' Gabi said later, leading the influx with a hot casserole dish wrapped in a teatowel. 'So I brought a kind of all-purpose vegetable dish I can put together in a matter of minutes.'

'And I just happened to have a frozen pavlova in my fridge, so that's my contribution,' Kirsten told him, follow-ing Gabi into the flat with the boxed dessert and acknowl-edging the introductions Gabi made.

Rory held the door, greeted the two male doctors who, waving bottles of wine, had followed their womenfolk, then, as no one else seemed to want to come in, closed it again.

It wasn't as if Alana had said she'd come, and if Daisy was right, and he felt instinctively that she probably was, then he certainly shouldn't be seeing any more of Alana than was absolutely necessary.

But as he watched Rosemary and Drusilla vie with each other for the hostess role he knew, even for Jason's sake, he couldn't marry either of them.

Though maybe he could go through some form of mar-riage—a set-up, not the real thing—until after the court case. Or indicate an intention to marry one of them soon. Would that work? His own solicitor might not approve of subterfuge, but he could ask Rosemary—which meant she'd know he intended doing it and would offer to be the pretend wife, then expect to be a real wife and he might just as well shoot himself right now...

'Are you OK?'

Josh asked the question, and Rory, after staring blankly at the man for a moment, nodded, then admitted grimly, 'Probably not, but, then, whoever is?'

Muttering things about food and kitchens, he walked away. He'd keep busy, pretend he was absolutely swamped by his hostly duties, and that way he wouldn't think about losing Jason, or Alana not coming, or pretend marriages or any of the other guff currently slamming around in his head.

He put plates out on the kitchen bench, added eating and serving utensils, clean glasses for the wine. What else? Napkins? Surely he had napkins. Jason had put away the groceries. He looked around for the boy, but couldn't see him, then the door opened and he came in, and close behind him was a tall, slim, tanned woman wearing what looked like a second skin, so closely did the dress slink down her body. The blonde hair—not a rat's-tail in sight—tumbled seductively around her shoulders, and he had a sudden image of it cascading down to brush his skin as he held her naked body on top of his own.

He closed his eyes, hoping she might be a mirage, but when he opened them she was still there, greeting her friends, chatting to Drusilla, turning to speak to Jason, who immediately left her side and crossed towards the kitchen.

'Alana cooked these,' he said, setting a clingfilm-wrapped plate of poppadoms on the bench. 'She said she's sorry she didn't have more to offer. You should give more notice, she said.'

He glanced over towards her, and felt a fiery rush of

desire so strong he wondered if a human body could self-combust.

'She brought this, too. Should I put it in the fridge?'

Jason's voice prompted reminders of Daisy's warning—used as an example according to Alana but still powerfully applicable to the situation.

'Thanks, mate,' Rory said. 'And ask her if she'd like a glass of that particular wine or the one that's already opened. You might take the bottle around and fill up any other glasses.'

That way I won't have to go near her, and have to fight the compulsion to touch the shining hair and skim my hands across the slinky dress.

Would his guests think he'd gone mad if he let out a loud groan?

Would taking Rosemary to bed—after all they'd been lovers right up until Alison had become ill—cure what ailed him?

Probably not, although the resultant complications could mean Drusilla would kill him. Then with his uncle dead and his aunt in gaol, Jason would have no one but his shifty, unreliable father—

'Can I give you a hand?'

Rory was so lost in his useless stream of conjecture that the voice startled him, and he turned to see the smiling redhead from the flat opposite the Grahams'. Kirsten—engaged to paediatrician Josh Phillips—friend of Alana's.

'I'm just going to put all the dishes on the bench and let people help themselves,' he told her. 'I was going quite well, then stalled at the cutlery stage.'

'Probably when Alana walked in,' Kirsten said in a kindly tone. 'I think all the men in the room stalled about then. Alex and Josh are so used to seeing her around the place in her uniform or gym clothes or tennis gear that they always do this open-mouth thing when she turns up dressed.'

'And you don't mind?' Rory asked, because personally, now this had been pointed out and he realised both men had gravitated to Alana, he'd have liked to have murdered both of them.

Kirsten, however, was smiling happily.

'I think I'd be more worried if Josh didn't notice her. After all, she's a very beautiful woman.'

Rory looked across the room—and nodded.

'She is that!' he said abruptly, then turned away, fussing quite unnecessarily with the big pot of curry. 'I think this is ready to serve. Shall we do it?'

From the far side of the room, Alana watched him moving about his kitchen, looking more masculine than ever in what might be considered a woman's domain.

She shouldn't have come, but Jason had tapped on her door—there to see if she was ready—and she hadn't been able to disappoint him. Seeing her friends as soon as she walked in the door had helped her overcome her initial trepidation, and a glass of wine had eased a little of her inner tension.

Two glasses of wine might be even better, but when Jason, circulating among the guests, tilted the bottle towards her, she shook her head. Two glasses might also unleash demons better kept on a very tight rein.

Then Jason filled it anyway, and grinned at her.

'If I fill it up for you then I can have a sip or two later,' he said, then the smile faded as he added with his usual inbred politeness, 'If that's all right with you, of course.'

Alana offered him a sip, which he took then grimaced.

'I think I'll stick to soft drink.'

'Come and get it!'

Kirsten called them to eat and in the shuffle that followed getting food and finding a seat, Alana ended up on a most uncomfortable couch, with Drusilla beside her.

'It'll be good for Jason to get back to school,' Drusilla said, the remark so seemingly innocuous that Alana agreed.

'Children his age need plenty to occupy their minds or they end up in trouble,' the 'child's' aunt continued, while Alana imagined Jason's reaction to being called a child.

'I told Rory that months ago. I wasn't in agreement about him taking time off school when Alison was ill, and I still feel he'd have got through the whole business better if he'd been made to follow his usual routine.'

Whole business? Was this woman talking about Jason's mother's death? Was that how she summed it up?

Biting back an urge to argue, she let Drusilla talk, listening with growing disbelief to some of the most ridiculous child-rearing theories she'd ever heard, until finally she was compelled to say, 'Jason is a teenager now. I don't think toddler taming techniques work for them.'

Drusilla fired a supercilious 'what would you know' look at Alana, who quickly ate the last bit of delicious curry and drained her wine. Then, knowing she was likely to explode if she had to listen to any more drivel, she stood up, saying, as politely as she could, 'I'd better take this plate into the kitchen.'

Where she found the host propped against the kitchen sink, surveying his visitors.

'Look,' she said, setting her plate down but keeping the wineglass and waving it towards him as she spoke. 'I realise you might have to get married in order to keep Jason, but for heaven's sake don't marry the aunt. The woman's got the weirdest ideas. Given even the slightest bit of control, she'd drive poor Jason batty in a week.'

'And what about me?' Rory asked, his blue eyes fixed on her face but totally unreadable.

'What *about* you?' Alana demanded crossly. Her body was cataloguing the man as if it didn't understand it wasn't allowed to be interested in him, and the catalogue points were having their usual effect on unreliable nerves and wayward flesh and rubberised bones.

'Don't I get some consideration in the marriage business?'

Alana frowned at him.

'I don't think so,' she said. 'After all, you'd be doing it for Jason, not yourself, though, of course, you'd have to live with the person, and in an adult-to-adult relationship, Drusilla mightn't be bad. I mean, I don't know her at all, it's just her child-rearing theories I've heard so far, which is why I'd worry about Jason.'

The inscrutable mask remained in place, but the rest of his body just *had* to be communicating with hers, Alana decided. As he'd said himself, it was too strong to be one-sided.

But it was no good being attracted to Rory Forrester…

'Perhaps I'd better go and sit with her again. Find out her thoughts on how a marriage should work.'

'And if she asks what you think?' Rory said quietly.

Alana felt a feather-light shiver touch her spine and wondered if they were still talking about Drusilla.

'I'd have to say I don't have any set ideas,' she said, while the hairs on the back of her neck prickled as if there were subtitles to everything they were saying. 'Apart from a vague notion of a partnership. My grandparents have had what I guess you'd call a traditional marriage—Pop worked and Nana stayed home—but, just seeing them together, you realise they're a team.'

She smiled, and found herself relaxing, just thinking about the loving couple who'd been so much part of her life. In fact, she'd go and visit them tomorrow. That should shake all the strange fancies out of her head.

'Special to you, are they?' Rory murmured, and when Alana looked up at him the mask had dropped, and there was a warmth and understanding in his eyes that stopped her breath.

'Hey, your glass is empty and I haven't been drinking it

so you must have. I'm going to open another bottle. I'll pour you one.'

Alana was so grateful for Jason's interruption she could have hugged him, but, aware a public hug would be as welcome to a teenager as chickenpox, she resisted the urge.

'I'll pass on the wine. I've a long drive tomorrow, and don't want a hangover for company.'

Jason, of course, asked where she was going, so she explained about her grandparents and their small property two hours' drive north of Westside.

'Your grandparents have goats and llamas? You're all animal-mad. I've never seen a llama—only in pictures or on TV—could I come?'

Rory's 'It's polite to be asked' came at the same time as Alana assured Jason she'd love the company. They moved away together, talking about arrangements, Alana pleased to be able to escape the effects of being in close proximity to Rory.

And genuinely happy at the thought of having Jason's company the following day. Her grandparents loved the company of young people.

The day cemented her friendship with Jason and reminded Alana of the solid foundations her mother's and grandparents' love had built into her own life.

She returned to work with a vigour that had been lacking recently, and an enthusiasm only slightly dimmed when the first doctor of the morning was Rory Forrester.

'I thought you'd be settling Jason into school,' she grumbled at him when he appeared, looking impossibly handsome for so early in the morning, as she finished taking over from the night sister.

'Not at seven-thirty! Even Drusilla wouldn't want him going off to school that early.'

Rory smiled at her, which made the impossibly handsome thing even worse, so, ignoring her reactions to both his presence and the smile, she scowled at him.

'Mr Cross is yours, I gather,' she said, deciding a professional approach was the only way to handle any awkwardness. 'Will you be running more tests on him today?'

'Yes, but I wanted to see him first. It's obvious he has a malfunction of his adrenal cortex, but I'd like to know what's causing it. We'll keep treating him for the adrenal crisis, and while he's still unstable, the stress factor is very important. If you can manage to keep him on his own, with as little disruption as possible—no lights, no visitors except his wife and you'll need to talk to her about not telling him anything that will upset him. The orders are on his chart— regular small meals, monitoring his fluid and food intake, his weight and his urine output.'

He sighed.

'He's one of those patients we'll probably be able to stabilise and who'd be able to continue leading a normal life, but with what's happening in his family, stress is unavoidable, so in the end he'll probably be in and out of here on a regular basis.'

'Family problems?' Alana asked, wondering how terrible they must be for someone with his own set to be sighing over them.

'You can't imagine! Have a talk to Mrs Cross when she comes in. Though I doubt even you could sort out her family.'

What's with this 'even you' stuff? Alana thought, but Rory was already moving towards Mr Cross's room so, like a dutiful charge nurse, she followed.

Mr Cross was stable, but confused about what had happened and not entirely happy about being in hospital.

'It's too much for my wife to be at home with all the mob. I should be there for her,' he told Rory, while Alana wondered how high anxiety levels could rise before they qualified as stress.

Rory spoke reassuringly to the man then took Alana's arm to steer her out of the room.

'Watch him closely and if you feel he's getting over-anxious, contact Ted. We might have to think about tran-quillisers of some kind, but I'd prefer not to while we're still conducting tests.'

He whisked away, leaving Alana with a warm patch of skin and a totally unacceptable feeling of desolation.

But the day had begun and she had plenty of work to do, including introducing a fresh-faced young student to the computer.

'Our ward secretary gets in at eight,' she told the young man—Craig Crain, according to his ID. 'She'll help you out if you get into a muddle, but I think you'll find it all pretty straightforward.'

She was surprised he'd actually materialised, because the memo that students would be typing up some patient rec-ords had only been emailed to all the internal medicine wards over the weekend.

Rory continued to prove he was no slouch in the organ-isation department, though the revived student rounds were taken by Ted, who explained that Rory was catching up on things he'd missed while introducing Jason to his new school.

Jason's induction into St Peter's became the topic of 'out of hospital' conversation among the inhabitants of Near West, as most of them had, by now, met the teenager and were keen to know how he got on.

'You'd think he'd been going there all his life,' Gabi said to Alana when they met at the local shop on Friday afternoon. 'He was telling me about the terrific tennis coach. His name was familiar but you know me, I don't know a tennis racket from a water-ski. Is he any good?'

'He's fantastic. He's the man I'd have recommended—not knowing he was working full time at the school. Jason's very lucky to have him.'

'He's talented, or so he tells me,' Gabi said, and Alana laughed.

'I suppose it's what they call the confidence of youth,' Alana said. 'Did we have it? In my mind, I was always so insecure I'd never have actually told anyone I was good at anything.'

'No, you wouldn't,' Gabi scoffed. 'You just did your shy retiring violet impersonation, then came out of the court and whopped anyone foolish enough to play against you. And you loved to win.'

'Only in sport,' Alana argued. 'I wouldn't have been so spineless in my relationship with Brian if I'd carried that competitive urge into my love life.'

'Wouldn't be so spineless about letting those women take over Rory Forrester either,' Gabi said, her attention seemingly focussed on choosing between two equally plump lettuces.

'What do you mean by that?' Alana demanded, removing one of the lettuces and plonking it back on the shelf. 'And don't you dare shrug as if it's something that just popped out of your mouth. I've known you long enough, Gabi Graham, to know nothing just pops out of your mouth. Every word is weighed and measured and every sentence plotted to the last full stop.'

Gabi shrugged anyway.

'And I know you just as well,' she reminded Alana, 'so don't tell me you're not interested in him.'

'Well, I'm not,' Alana blustered, then, because the whole situation was so impossible she had to tell someone, she blurted out the rest of it. 'And even if I was, Daisy says it can't happen. She says it would be disastrous for Jason, and he's got to be Rory's first concern at the moment, and you know I like the kid, so he's my concern as well.'

Gabi's wide brown eyes grew even wider at this gabble of information.

She touched Alana's arm.

'Perhaps we need a coffee,' she said. 'Finish your shopping then I'll shout.'

Alana glanced at her watch, then pulled a mournful face.

'It's definitely what I need—girl-talk—but Jason'll be home from school and he was having his first session with the tennis coach today and wanted a practice when he got home. I just ducked down because we're out of juice. You can't believe how much kids his size can put away.'

She patted Gabi's small neat bulge of pregnancy.

'You stay right there, little one,' she said. 'It's cheaper that way.'

They parted, but as Gabi queued at the checkout she watched her friend stride briskly back towards Near West. Though Alana would never admit it, her relationship with Brian had left her wary and defensive of all men. Now, of all the unlikely people, Rory Forrester had penetrated those defences, but to what end?

Even Gabi knew enough psychology to see how Jason, already forced to adjust to so many life changes, could be affected by a relationship between his uncle and the woman he saw as his own particular friend.

CHAPTER TEN

'KEEPING the drinks and snack foods for Jason is one thing,' Alana complained to Gabi a week later, when they'd finally got together for their cup of coffee. At Alana's flat, not the coffee-shop, because Jason was getting ready to go to a school social and had told Alana he'd need her there to check he looked OK. 'But keeping up with him on the tennis court is becoming impossible. Alex plays. I might conscript him some time this weekend, and the pair of us can take Jason on.'

'Doesn't Rory play?' Gabi asked, and Alana, knowing Gabi could read her too well, turned away.

'Oh, love,' Gabi said gently, reaching out to touch Alana lightly on the shoulder. 'You do know how to complicate your life, don't you?'

Alana nodded, then shrugged.

'It's not as if I did it deliberately,' she muttered, but Gabi was obviously putting herself into Alana's place—imagining how she must feel.

'How do you manage at work? You must see him every day. Feeling as you obviously do, how do you handle it?'

'I'm fantastic!' Alana told her, smiling in spite of the dump-truck load of sadness in her chest. 'You've no idea how efficient being lovesick can make you. I positively breeze through my work—that's the keeping-busy remedy—then I nag at others to do better so they all argue and mutter at me—that's the expend-your-emotions-on-something-else cure. The ward is running like a well-oiled machine, the patients have learned to lie straight in their beds—and I even got the window cleaners in, and you know how hard that is at Royal Westside. I think they spend most of their time cleaning the windows in the executive offices because there are so many secretaries in short skirts working on that floor.'

'And Rory?'

'He probably appreciates short-skirted secretaries as much as the next man,' Alana replied, sounding as offhand as she could manage when, in fact, the situation between them had reached the stage where Alana sometimes wondered if lightning might suddenly crack and sizzle in the air between them with the tension in the atmosphere around them so tight. 'And he's almost certainly got clean windows.'

She hesitated, then said quietly, 'He's probably got to get married, you know. Both Drusilla and Rosemary are hanging around in anticipation of that fact. If he had a normal job—one where he worked regular hours and could arrange stable supervision for Jason during those hours— then, even though he's single, he'd probably win the custody case. But part of his job is being on call, and no judge is going to be happy about a thirteen-year-old left alone in a flat as often as it's likely to happen.'

'Custody?' Gabi breathed the word. 'I knew he was worrying about something—he was asking Alex last weekend who he might approach about lecturing work. But who's fighting him for custody?'

Alana hesitated. She shouldn't have mentioned the problem, but Gabi was her best friend and if she didn't talk to someone she'd explode.

'Jason's father. Apparently he remarried as soon as Alison died, possibly so he could put himself in the forefront of the custody battle.'

'But thirteen-year-olds are old enough to choose,' Gabi protested. 'Surely Jason would choose to live with Rory.'

'He would—it's what he wants, but it's still up to the judge to decide if that choice means he'll be living in a safe environment. Rory's solicitors say that going in with a story that he's going to be married very soon won't be good enough, because the court will want to speak to the woman and gauge her relationship with Jason. If he goes the marriage route, it's going to have to be with a particular woman—and either be already married to her or at least about to be. If he opts out of the marriage scenario altogether then loses Jason because he's single...'

'How do you know all this if you and Rory barely see each other outside work?'

Alana sighed.

'Rosemary kindly filled me in on some of it, then Rory— well, we do see each other all the time, really, because he comes down with Jason some evenings and calls for him at times when I'm here.'

She paused then added defensively, 'He has to talk to someone, and he knows I care about the kid.'

'Of course you do,' Gabi said, 'but it still seems weird to me that the father would even bother.'

Not wanting to bring up Jason's theory that money lay behind the claim, Alana skirted the issue.

'I phoned a cousin of Brian's—that's how desperate I am—who works in the family court to find out about how these things are likely to be decided. It's not good, Gabi.'

'But it can't be hopeless either,' Gabi said, with the stout determination that had helped her survive and overcome a miscarriage and a separation from her husband. 'What about a housekeeper? Someone living in who's there when Rory's called out?'

'He's thought of that, but it would mean getting a bigger flat or house, and even live-in housekeepers have days off. Anyway, when he mentioned it to Jason, it struck more rocks as Jason hated the idea, taking it as a lack of trust on Rory's part that he thought Jason needed someone watching over him.'

'Yes, at his age, I can see his point.' Gabi nodded. 'Teenage indestructibility! But there must be another answer.'

'Must there?' Alana said, getting up to answer a now recognisable knock on her front door. 'This is Rory now,' she said warningly to Gabi. 'He's come to take Jason to the social. Not a word.'

'As if I would!' Gabi's protest was indignant, which didn't mean she wouldn't spill the beans in a trice if she thought it would achieve something.

'Alana, help! I've put that stuff in my hair, and it's all going to fall out. I'm going to be bald. I can't go out bald. Bald, bald, bald!'

Jason's screeching eruption out of the bathroom held them all spellbound, and though Alana did step forward and put out her hand as if to stop him, he was now dancing around the room, clutching his head.

'Stop! Stand still! Tell us what stuff.'

Rory took control and his brisk orders did at least slow Jason's panicky capering.

'Some stuff—in a white bottle. It's a defoliation thing—like Agent Orange,' Jason wailed. 'We were learning about that in history. They sprayed it on the trees in Vietnam in a war and all the leaves fell off, so it's sure to happen to hair.'

He turned accusing eyes on Alana and added, 'Why would you have something like that beside the shower? I thought it was conditioner.'

'There is no Agent Orange in my bathroom,' Alana said firmly. 'But even if there was, just what would you be doing, using it? Haven't we had this conversation, Jason McAllister? What's mine is yours anywhere in this flat *except* the bathroom, where what's mine is mine! *My* toothbrush, *my* toothpaste, *my* shampoo, *my* exfoliating lotion, Jason. *Ex*-, not de-. It gets rid of old skin cells, not hair, but it's gritty so I bet you feel as if there's sand in your hair. Come here and let me look.'

Gabi was surprised to see the teenager first quieten, then

stop his bouncing around and finally, a picture of contrition, step obediently towards Alana and bend his head.

'Ha! Grit. I'm taking samples and I'll send them to the lab as proof positive you've been in my things.'

She ruffled his hair and, as he straightened, she gave him a gentle shove.

'Hurry back into the shower and rinse it out, then, just this once, you can use my conditioner, which is in the *blue* bottle on the shelf. And you'd better hurry or you're going to be late.'

But if Gabi was surprised by her friend's placid handling of the situation, so too was Rory Forrester, by the look of him.

He was staring at the doorway where Jason had disappeared, then he turned back to Alana and a worried frown gathered on his forehead, as if he wasn't sure who she was.

'What? What's wrong?' Alana felt the full impact of the frowning look. 'Are you upset I yelled at him? Do you think he should get away with stuff like that? Daisy said to treat him like a person. If you'd used my shampoo I'd have yelled at you.'

'You didn't yell, you were just firm,' Gabi said, and Alana had to smile. Since they'd been four, they'd been rushing to each other's defence.

But in spite of Gabi's soothing words, Rory was still frowning, which was altering Alana's usual response-to-Rory mechanisms. Exaggerating them somehow. So, instead of being a shaky, shivery, practically slavering but having to hide it mess, she was a *defensive*, shaky, shivery, practically slavering but having to hide it mess.

'Well?' she said—that was the defensive bit coming out.

He shook his head and continued to look at her, and if anything the frown deepened, while his lips took on a grim, set line.

'Jason will be a while. I'm going to pop over and see Daisy,' he said, whipping out the door so quickly neither

Alana nor Gabi had time to tell him Daisy would be at work.

Although—Alana checked the time—maybe she wouldn't have left yet.

Jason finally reappeared, his hair carefully arranged into a kind of roughness usually consistent with having just got out of bed. Then gelled into place, apparently, for when Alana touched it, the spiky bits pricked her fingers.

She grinned at him.

'For someone who complained about a bit of my exfoliating lotion in their hair, you've added plenty of foreign matter of your own.'

'It's the look,' he told her. 'You've got to get with it, man!'

He cuffed Alana lightly on the upper arm—she'd learned to duck most of the time—then looked around. 'Where's Rory?'

'He slipped over to see Daisy,' Gabi told him, and Alana, who'd been studying him as she often did, picking out features which reminded her of Rory, saw his lips tighten in a way that rarely happened these days.

'I'm getting myself sorted. I don't need to see Daisy,' he growled.

'Why assume he's gone to see Daisy about you, Mr I'm-the-centre-of-the-universe?' Alana said. 'Maybe he's gone to see her for himself? As a friend, not a customer. He's allowed to have friends.'

Jason rolled his eyes.

'Do they all have to be women?'

Exactly, Alana thought, but she didn't say it.

'How *are* things upstairs?' Gabi asked the question Alana always avoided. 'I'm surprised one of those women hasn't killed the other by now or Rory killed both of them. The flats aren't really big enough for three adults to live comfortably together.'

'Drusilla might have gone, but when Rosemary came,

she decided she'd better stick it out. They've both got this idea Rory needs to be married, though it beats me why any man would want a woman in his life for ever. They're nothing but trouble.'

'Thanks, Jase,' Alana said, and watched his ears go pink with embarrassment.

'Not you,' he assured her. 'You're more like a man. You don't fuss over things, or try to boss me, or mother me, or make me talk about stuff.' He smiled approvingly at Alana. 'You're like a mate!'

Alana knew this was the highest compliment Jason could pay, and while her heart treasured it, it also ached with the knowledge that it was one more indication Daisy had been right in her reading of the situation. A shift in the dynamics of her relationship with Rory would obviously be, in Jason's eyes, a betrayal of his friendship.

She turned away to blink back unexpected moisture in her eyes, while Jason went to the front door and opened it, no doubt to go in search of his missing uncle, returning only to poke his head through the door to announce, 'We're off!'

'Have fun,' Alana and Gabi chorused, then, as they heard the ping on the lift doors closing, Alana sank into a chair, looked at her friend and smiled.

'See how it is?'

Gabi nodded.

'But all he needs is time. Once he's settled and secure, surely then he's not going to resent Rory and you getting together.'

'Who knows what might have happened?' Alana replied. 'It's not something that's going to be put to the test, Gabi. Rory was told to expect an early date for the custody hearing, possibly as soon as next week. And part of it could be a psychological evaluation of Jason. If they go into it with any hint that Jason might be emotionally unstable then Rory stands a good chance of losing the case.'

She sighed. 'It's just too horrible to contemplate.'

'But the father never saw the boy—why should he have rights?'

Alana sighed again.

'He can argue that Alison never allowed contact and that he didn't take her to court because he thought it would be harmful for the boy to have two parents squabbling over him. The unexploded bomb in all of this is that if Rory decides to get married but chooses Rosemary over Drusilla, which is logical as they've already had a relationship, then Drusilla will probably swap sides and back her brother in his lies. A woman scorned and all that.'

'Maybe he needs a third option,' Gabi mused. 'I wonder what Daisy would say to a marriage of convenience?'

The thought of one of her friends marrying Rory made Alana feel nauseous, so she changed the subject, asking Gabi how she was enjoying the Children's Hospital, talking shop in an effort to block out her heartache.

Jason's second week at school proved even better than his first. He developed a special friendship.

'And he's asked me to stay this weekend,' he told Alana. 'His father builds go-carts and there's a big go-cart race this weekend so I could go to that with them.'

They were both involved in the Thursday cage clean, and excitement bubbled out of him, like champagne froth from a hastily opened bottle.

'It means I'll miss cleaning out the animals on Saturday because I'll go straight from school on Friday and go back to school with him on Monday.'

The radiance dimmed slightly as he added, 'You don't mind? You'll be OK here on your own?'

Alana assured him she'd manage, and though she should have felt relief that she'd be getting her old life back, if only for a weekend, what actually struck her was that she'd miss having him around.

Although there *was* a concert on Saturday night.

But even that failed to thrill—she'd keep looking at the empty seat and imagining Rory there.

Funny how he hadn't ever recognised her…

Though perhaps he had and hadn't said anything—just as she hadn't said anything to him…

Or maybe it hadn't been him at all, you great dope!

As usual these days, her head was arguing with itself—and getting nowhere.

'Hey, I've just put clean paper in that cage.' Jason's protest jolted her back to what she was supposed to be doing.

'Is this weekend away OK with Rory? Has he spoken to the people involved—Marcus, isn't that your friend's name? Has Rory spoken to his parents?'

'Rory talked to them last night and he met them at the school. Marcus started late, like me. It was just lucky we ended up in most of the same classes. He'd been at another school, but when they shifted house to be closer to the go-cart track, he had to change.'

'You'll have to pack tonight,' Alana reminded. 'Just make sure you have enough clothes for the whole weekend and a clean school shirt for Monday.'

'I know that stuff,' Jason told her, and she had to agree. He was far more self-sufficient than she had been at the same age.

Alana left for work before Jason was up the following morning, and returned home to a flat that seemed intolerably empty. If it hadn't been for the concert, she'd have packed up herself and gone to her grandparents' for the weekend. Looking on the bright side, a Friday night had been restored to her, and she could spend most of it in a deep bubble bath, with a glass of wine and a good book.

Boring!

She did it anyway, and spent Saturday on necessary grocery shopping then seeking out the perfect pair of shoes to go with an outfit she'd only worn once, to the wedding of a cousin she didn't like.

The stilted, stifling occasion had put her off the softly fitted trousers and silky black top but, trying them on the previous night, they'd looked good, and she'd decided to get some mileage out of them.

The rest of the day was spent avoiding the phone, though forty-seven times she'd weakened and walked towards it, thinking a casual call to Rory to find out if he was going to the concert couldn't be misconstrued as anything else.

But each time she'd resisted. He'd wonder about her sanity if she suddenly phoned to ask if he'd sat next to her in a concert a whole month ago.

Or if he intended going again tonight!

Of course, she realised as she was picking her way carefully towards her seat that evening, then looked up and saw him there, she was going to feel even more stupid if it did turn out to be him—it was—and she hadn't asked.

'I thought it might have been you.'

A duet of the words, soprano and bass.

'Why didn't you say something?' Alana.

'Did you know and not say?' Rory's line.

Then they simply looked at each other, and all the skittish emotional vibes Alana had been battling for a month burst their floodgates, and with a soft, 'Oh Rory,' she leaned forward and kissed him very gently on the lips.

They were close enough for her to feel a shudder rip through his body, for her ears to catch the echo of a despairing groan. Then he touched her lips with his finger—a don't-speak kind of gesture—and took her hand, holding it tightly in his, his thumb running over her skin, telling her all kinds of things his lips could never say.

And right then, with the violins tuning up in the least melodious manner, she knew that tonight would be their night. A one-off, one and only, but theirs no matter what. Had he sensed her thoughts that his fingers tightened, that he changed hands and put his free arm around her shoulders?

On her other side, Mrs Schnitzerling must be puce with outrage over such licentious behaviour at a concert, but it felt so good—so right. Alana rested her head against Rory's arm and gave herself up not only to the music but to the mind-blowing delight of enjoying it with Rory.

'Do you want a drink—stretch your legs?' he asked, when the intermission lights came on.

'Not really,' Alana told him. Was he mad? Getting up and going out to the foyer would mean letting go of his hand and losing the heavy arm around her shoulders—the fingers that had fiddled with her hair while the music and his presence had swamped her soul with happiness.

'Strange that,' he said, turning and pressing his lips against her cheek. 'Neither do I.'

So they sat, saying nothing, but Alana guessed he might also be feeling some of the elation buzzing in her body. And some of the very sexual tension that was rising to tightening the muscles in her abdomen, making her nipples harden and peak into tiny nubs of longing.

Tension that could only be released one way...

With Jason away, her flat was entirely hers. They'd have tonight—possibly tomorrow night as well. Then—

'The custody hearing's set down for Wednesday.' Rory put her thoughts into words.

'So we've got tonight.'

She felt Rory stiffen, and saw the shock in his eyes as he turned towards her.

'You're saying?' he demanded hoarsely.

'That at least we'd have something to remember—to hold onto. That we'd at least have one night...'

She couldn't go on—the idea was too difficult to put into words.

'Come on!' He hauled her to her feet. 'We can hear Dvorak any time. We're going home.'

Alana knew she was trembling because she could barely organise her legs enough to walk sideways out along the row of seats, but Rory's hand sustained her and somehow she made it to the end.

Where Mr and Mrs Schnitzerling were waiting to edge back to their seats.

'Medical emergency,' Alana said to them, though she was blushing so furiously they probably didn't believe her.

'Did you drive here?' Rory demanded, still striding out and towing Alana behind him like a boat tender.

'No, I hate the parking. I always get a bus and cab it home.'

'Good. I've got my car.'

They were out of the theatre now, charging along a city footpath.

'Just around here.'

Car lights flashed as he used a remote to unlock the navy saloon, then he opened the passenger door, almost thrust Alana inside, strode around the bonnet and slumped in beside her.

'Hell! I didn't think I'd make it,' he said, flopping his head back against the headrest for a moment. 'I thought I'd have to ravish you right there and then. Talk about an agonising month! Seeing you every day—seeing Jason joking and laughing with you, wanting to kill him because he was close to you and I wasn't.'

He paused for a moment then turned to her and added, 'And even now I daren't kiss you—I'm terrified of even touching you—in case the dam walls burst and I end up behaving like a sex-crazed adolescent in the front seat of the car.'

Sexual heat and hysterical laughter vied for supremacy in Alana, the laughter winning, though she risked a touch, reaching out to clasp her hand around Rory's fingers and squeeze them in silent apology.

'I'm sorry,' she said, when she'd finally recovered

enough breath to speak. 'But it's so stupid, the whole thing. First we sit next to each other at a concert, and neither of us mention it for a month, then this—this together thing—rushing out of the theatre because we can't wait to get to bed. It's like some crazy romantic comedy.'

'Except it isn't funny,' Rory said quietly, then he started the car and eased out from the kerb.

Was it her laughter that had killed the mood between them?

Alana didn't know. All she knew was that she wanted him, and if she couldn't have him for ever, which would be any living, breathing woman's first choice, then she'd make do with one night.

Perhaps two?

Rory tried to concentrate on driving, but it wasn't difficult enough to keep his mind off any segment of the dog's breakfast that was currently his life. He doubted microsurgery on a newborn's heart would have been complicated enough to blank out *his* problems.

The most prominent of which, right now, apart from a bit of his anatomy, was the woman sitting right beside him.

Over the past month Alana Wright had shifted from being a thorn in his side at work, and a woman to whom he was attracted, into the only person in the world who occupied his thoughts as much as Jason did. And occupied his body even more!

The more he saw and learnt of her, the more he realised she was the woman of his dreams—or would have been had he ever been foolish enough to indulge in such fancies. She was bright, beautiful, intelligent, efficient at her job, an expert in handling patients, as well as the friend and confidante Jason needed at this time in his life.

The realisation that he loved her had come to him in such a blinding flash—had it only been a week ago that he'd been waiting to take Jason to the school social and had watched Alana handle the lad's extreme teenage reactions so calmly? He'd had to mumble an excuse about see-ing Daisy and get out of the room, needing time to consider the implications.

Time to accept the impossibility of it all!

'We shouldn't even be thinking about this,' he said. 'It will only make things harder.'

'I know,' she said—he'd forgotten to add 'attuned to his thoughts' to his list of her attributes.

'So we shouldn't?'

He didn't look at her—couldn't—simply steered the car carefully down the drive at Near West, inserted the card to open the garage security grill, then watched the grill rise as if it were the most fascinating sight in the world.

'Of course we shouldn't,' Alana said, and his gut con-tracted with the blow. 'But let's do it anyway. We're both mature, consenting adults. Look at it as a last fling before marriage. It's not as if you'd be cheating on either one of your women—or would you?'

The question caught him as he was reversing into his parking space, and he messed up the angle and had to pull out to try again.

'I don't know how you could even think that—let alone ask it,' he said savagely. 'As if I could—with either of them—when a long-haired blonde is driving me insane with the kind of desire I didn't think thirty-something-year-olds could possibly experience.'

She smiled at him, then, as he turned off the engine, took his hand, lifted it to his lips and pressed a kiss into the palm.

His skin tingled and his body jolted back to attention. The 'should we', 'shouldn't we' argument hammered in his head, but he'd stopped listening. He squeezed her fingers in a silent promise that he'd soon be holding them again and positively leapt out of the car. He was around the boot in time to catch the passenger door as she swung it open, and hold it for her as she climbed out.

Long, long legs in slinky black trousers that clung to them, then she was standing beside him, shadowy breasts revealed in the V of her demure black top.

'Alana!' He barely breathed her name, his chest so tight with tension it was hurting.

'Upstairs,' she whispered, brushing her lips against his. 'And cross your fingers, toes and anything else crossable that there's no one in the lift or in my foyer or anywhere else along the way.'

'We could walk up,' he suggested.

'And be exhausted when we get there?' Her laughter rippled in the air around him, making him feel light-headed with excitement.

The lift doors opened, and they stepped into the empty cubicle.

'If anyone gets in on the ground floor I'll go up and come back down,' Rory murmured as they stood, circumspectly apart, while the lift rose.

Past the ground floor, stopping on two—no one in sight.

'Stupid, isn't it?' Alana said, then she swept away the maudlin sentimentality threatening to overwhelm her and unlocked her door.

Rory must have guessed how she felt, for no sooner had he shut the door behind her than he took her in his arms and held her close. An asexual embrace of total comfort.

'It's not stupid when you consider why we're doing it— why we're being cautious and secretive. If we want this night, that's how it has to be, my beautiful Alana. But I've brought you enough unhappiness—by putting you in this position—so it's up to you to decide if you want to take it further, or say goodnight and we'll never mention it again.'

'I can't imagine not taking it further,' she said, pushing out the words that held equal measures of love and despair. 'But it has to be our night—with no thought for the future, no mention of other options, nothing but the joy of giving pleasure to each other.'

She felt his heart thump against his chest as he held her even more tightly, then, as their bodies' subliminal messages grew more urgent, he kissed her and she shifted so her lips replied with all the passionate longing she'd kept leashed for so long.

Words no longer necessary, they clung to each other, lips and hands exploring, heated murmurs encouraging, giving and receiving promises of the pleasure to come.

'Have you decided what to do about the custody case?' Alana asked as, replete at last, they lay, limbs tangled together, exhausted but not willing to waste time with sleep. 'About the marriage thing?'

'Marriage thing!' Rory repeated, with a huff of bitter laughter. 'That's all it will be—a thing, a bit of paper. What I can't believe is that either Rosemary or Drusilla would want to do it. They both know I'm not in love with them.'

'But if you marry, you should do it properly,' Alana said, tightening her arms around his chest. 'For Jason's sake, make a proper go of it. Imagine how terrible it would be for him to grow up knowing you're unhappy.'

Rory pressed a kiss against her forehead.

'How can I do it properly when I love you?' he said, his voice so husky with emotion she shivered in the warmth of his embrace. 'It wouldn't only be me going into a loveless marriage—I'd be dooming either Drusilla or Rosemary to one as well. No, Alana, I know I've been dithering about it, and listening to too many people's advice, but I think I've got to risk going to the hearing as I am and admitting I'm likely to remain single for some time.'

'But if you lose?'

There was silence for a moment, then he moved away from her, sitting up on the edge of the bed and leaning forward, elbows on knees, his head propped on his hands.

'I can't even contemplate it,' he said. Then he turned and kissed her.

'And now I've got to go. It's late but not so late I mightn't have been at a bar or club after the concert. I daren't make matters worse than they already are by spending the night with you. I can't afford to give the opposition any ammunition to use against me, and both Rosemary and Drusilla would become the opposition if they thought it would help their cause.'

He shook his head and an odd smile twitched across his lips.

'That sounds appallingly conceited, doesn't it? As if I fancy myself as irresistible to women. But it's not me, it's the money that attracts them. Jason told you about it. It's quite a lot.' There was a pause before he added with a bitterness she'd never heard in him before, 'For what it's worth.'

She sat up to kiss him, and he gathered her into his arms.

'The worst of it, for me, is the pain I'm causing you, when all you've done is open your loving heart to a boy who needed a friend. And this is how I reward you!'

Alana tried to speak but couldn't. Rory's voice had cracked as he'd spoken—but if she opened her lips it would be a full-blooded wail that would come out, not just a little cracking noise.

She watched him dress, touched the hand he held out to her in farewell, then, as she heard the front door of her flat close, she turned her face into the pillow and wept.

They still had one more night.

That was the first thought that surfaced in Alana's head the following morning. Then reality crashed through. They'd spent part of one night together and already she ached with missing him. Her fingers clenched against the need to touch him.

After two nights?

She'd be a besotted mess and it would be obvious to

everyone who came within a mile of her, so she was better off with the one night and getting over it.

Ha! Big joke, that.

She climbed out of bed, showered and dressed in comfortable weekend cut-off jeans and T-shirt, then drifted around the empty flat for five minutes before deciding she couldn't bear the loneliness.

She was telling the parrot about her problems when the phone rang. Grateful for any interruption—the parrot was the most unsympathetic animal she knew—she answered it, rather than letting the machine censor the call.

'Alex's working and I've come up the road for breakfast. I've got the papers and a table. You'll join me?'

'I'll be right there—just as soon as I've fed Stubby.'

Of course, as soon as she'd agreed she realised how stupid she'd been. Gabi had extra-sensory perception when it came to relationships. Unless Alana could put on a really good act, she'd guess something had happened. And much as Alana might want to talk it all through with her best friend, she wasn't ready to share either the joy or the pain just yet.

But she'd said yes, so she set off.

Once outside, the brightness of the morning made her wish even more fervently that she'd stayed at home. It was a be-happy day and she didn't fit in it. She needed an overcast, drizzling, be-miserable day.

She decided to ignore it—to pretend the sun wasn't shining like a light of hope in the cerulean sky. What was cerulean anyway, and why did people talk about sky that way?

'If you keep frowning like that, he'll think you don't want to see him.'

Gabi's voice startled her, and she looked across the pavement to where her friend sat at a table in the shade of the striped awning.

With Rory by her side?

'I'm protective colouring. Kirsten's here, too—she's ordering. Josh is helping his mother do something revolting to the horses.'

'And Rory just happened along?' Alana said, telling herself she definitely wasn't pleased with this development, in spite of the fact that it was *so* good to see him.

'No, I made him come.' Gabi sounded inordinately pleased with herself.

'You *made* him come?'

'Well, I met him at the paper shop and suggested he join us. His house guests are still in bed, and even if they do wake up and come prowling around, they won't be able to object to him having breakfast with *three* women. Safety in numbers and all that.'

She pulled out a chair and indicated to Alana to sit.

Next to Rory, who waited until she'd subsided into it before touching her lightly on the arm.

'I'll go if you're uncomfortable,' he said quietly.

She covered his hand with hers.

'I am, but if you go I'll shoot you,' she muttered, then circumspectly withdrew her hand but let it drop to rest on his knee beneath the table.

'The thing is,' Gabi began. 'Kirsten and I—you know you can't keep anything from Kirsten, Alana—well, we've been talking and it seems that you're both being far too negative about all this.'

Alana glanced at Rory, wondering how he was going to take a couple of women interfering in his life.

'Don't worry, Alana, we've already told Rory we're working on it.' Kirsten had returned, and she smiled brightly at Alana then answered her unspoken question. 'He tried to be very stand-offish at first but we've broken him down. Once he realised he needed us, what could he do?'

'He needed you?' Alana said weakly, glancing at Rory and catching a smile that made her pulse race.

'Well, he could hardly have had breakfast with you this

morning if we hadn't been here, now, could he?' Kirsten demanded.

Alana shook her head, and Gabi, perhaps realising how lost she was feeling, took pity on her and said, 'Sit down, Kirsten, and shut up while I explain.'

Kirsten sat and Gabi turned to Alana.

'We've been talking about it and Kirsten's been talking to Drusilla and Rosemary.'

'Relationship espionage?' Rory murmured, but Alana was too lost to laugh.

'Both of them say they're only staying for the custody case. I know Drusilla mentioned renting a flat in Near West, but Madeleine says it won't be available for ages—'

'Bribery and corruption?'

Gabi shot Rory a scathing glare and continued her explanation.

'So Drusilla will go back to Sydney, too, and if they don't make a move once it's over, then you'll have to show some spine and kick them out, Rory.'

'I'll get you to help me,' he promised gravely, and though a smile flashed across his lips, his eyes remained serious, and Alana knew he was thinking not of the women, who'd been troublesome, but of Jason, who was his prime concern.

'So, you get custody of Jason, the women depart, and with our help—'

'Whoa!' Rory interrupted Kirsten's part of the story. 'I get custody of Jason? Nice as it is of you to award it, it's up to a judge.'

Alana heard the tightness in his voice and pressed her fingers deeper into his thigh, hoping to offer comfort and reassurance.

'You will,' Kirsten told him. 'That's what we've sorted out. We thought we could all come to court, or as many of us from the flats who are available could come, and explain to the judge that although you might not have a wife right now, you were living in a community of caring people where there would always be someone available to keep an eye on Jason. Gabi's only working part time, Madeleine or Ingrid are always at home in the penthouse, Daisy's home during the day, and Alana and I, and the Grahams, and often Josh, are there at night. You programme all our numbers into your phone, with a list for Jason, and in an emergency all he has to do is hit buttons until he gets someone. After all, it was Alex who phoned the fire brigade then found you to let you know what was happening the night he got stuck on the ledge.'

Rory shook his head, while sudden light dawned in Alana's head. He'd left the concert a month ago because Jason had been stuck on a ledge!

'You'd all do that for me?' Rory said, sounding so bemused Alana had to squeeze his leg again.

Kirsten grinned at him.

'No, but we do like the kid!' she teased. 'Anyway, with that fixed up, I really can't see any reason, if you take it slowly, why you and Alana can't continue seeing each other.'

This time she grinned at Gabi. 'See, I put that very discreetly. I didn't say "continue your affair", did I? Gabi says I can't be discreet,' she added to Rory, flashing him a luminous smile. 'And she keeps making doubtful noises when I mention this part of the plan, but I think it would work.'

She paused, and Alana, knowing Kirsten, wondered what outrageous suggestion was coming.

'We'll be decoys and Jason-minders and make sure he's happy doing other things so you two can have time to yourselves, and eventually, once he's settled down... Well, I thought I'd leave the rest to you.'

Alana looked at Kirsten. She was obviously so pleased with the plan it was hard to throw cold water on it, but in her aching, heavy heart Alana knew it wouldn't work.

'I've never been too sure of what the word meant, but to me it sounds like what they call a clandestine affair,' she said, then she shook her head. 'I don't think so, Kirsten. It's the clandestine part. I might not know what it means, but it still smacks of sneaky and underhanded, and love isn't meant to be that way.'

She looked at Rory, trying to gauge how he might be reacting to this desperate scheming, then realised it didn't matter how he reacted, it still felt wrong to her.

'I couldn't do it,' she said bluntly, 'because it would spoil something beautiful, and it would also be deceiving Jason when he needs it least.'

'Oh, hell, I hadn't thought of that!' Kirsten faltered. 'The deceiving-Jason part of it. No, you couldn't do it. I can see that now.'

She looked at Gabi and sighed.

'Now we'll have to think of something else!'

Which was when Rory laughed, and as the rich, deep, melodious sound rolled over her, Alana knew her heart was breaking.

CHAPTER ELEVEN

SOMEHOW Alana sat through breakfast, quietly enjoying just being near Rory, while Kirsten came up with outrageous suggestions, keeping Rory amused with her nonsense, and Gabi smiled but behind the smile was still thinking of possible solutions to the dilemma.

'There isn't one,' she murmured to her friend, when Rory, insisting it was his shout, got up to pay the bill, and Kirsten, arguing it was her idea they all eat together, went with him to fight over it.

'There has to be,' Gabi said, displaying the same dogged determination that had got her onto the helicopter rescue team in spite of a desperate fear of heights and flying. 'Maybe when Jason's older…'

'Maybe,' Alana agreed, but deep inside she knew if they didn't end things cleanly, frustration would gnaw away at both their feelings and diminish the power of the emotions they'd felt for each other.

Rory and Kirsten returned, still arguing, and though Rory's eyes sought and found Alana's, when they began the walk back to the flats, it was Gabi who walked beside him.

With tennis practice after school, Jason was late home on Monday, going directly to Rory's flat for his dinner. Conscious of how much she'd missed him, Alana waited, then, as he walked in, was hard pushed to resist the urge to give him a 'welcome home' hug.

He dropped his bag on the floor in the centre of the living room, then grinned at her.

'Marcus reckons it must be cool to have two homes,' he

said, looking around as if checking she hadn't changed anything in his absence. 'And could he have one of the guinea pigs next time Biddy has babies?'

He chatted on, answering questions about his weekend, telling her technical things she didn't understand about go-carts, talking and joking, until it became obvious there was something he wasn't saying.

'What's up?' she said quietly, sitting down because she knew she probably wouldn't like what he had to tell her.

'Rory's heard from his solicitor. I have to go to court on Wednesday.'

'Are you worried about it?'

'Yes.'

'Did he tell you a number of tenants in the flats are going with you—or sending declarations if we can't get there—to say we'll all keep an eye on you if ever Rory's called out? That's if you want us to be like extra guardians for you.'

For a moment she thought she'd said the wrong thing, but when she saw him swallow, and his ears turn pink, she knew it was emotion keeping him silent.

He bent over and picked up his bag and turned away from her, saying, as he left the room, 'I'll put my stuff away. I left the dirty things upstairs. I guess after Wednesday I'll have to move back up.'

Stopped and turned.

'But we'll still be friends, won't we?'

She smiled at him, found herself swallowing as well, then managed, 'Of course we will, you idiot!'

As he turned away the second time, she saw his shoulders relax, and knew Jason, at least, was OK for the moment.

Though by Wednesday, everyone was so nervous that tempers were flaring without warning. Kirsten, who'd asked for and been given the day off, rang before seven to remonstrate with Alana that she hadn't done likewise.

'It's not too late. Call in sick,' Kirsten suggested, and Alana snapped.

'It *is* too late and I really don't think Rory and Jason want the whole circus troupe of Near West residents in court with them. The solicitor said you might not even get in to say your piece, though the judge will look at depositions. And I've done mine.'

She slammed the phone down then looked up to see a pyjama-clad Jason standing in the doorway.

'Don't you care what happens to me, then?' he said, and Alana felt shock rocket through her body.

'Of course I care,' she told him, then she crossed the room and gave him a hug. 'More than you will ever know. I want whatever's best for you, and in my opinion you're old enough to know that for yourself. If you want to stay with Rory then, as far as I'm concerned, that's how the judge should decide. I won't be there, but my promise to always be here for you is on a piece of paper and the judge will read that with all the others. And I'll be thinking about you all day, and I'm even going to give you my mobile phone so as soon as you come out you can ring me to tell me what happened. Just turn it off while you're in court.'

She'd stepped away from him after the hug, but had stayed close, so when she finished her little pep talk she was still within reach of the long, undeveloped arms which reached out to hug her back.

'Thanks!' he whispered, and bumped his head against hers to ease a little of the emotional tension strung between them.

'I'll get the phone,' Alana said, and was heading for her handbag when there was a knock on the door.

She knew it was Rory before she opened it—not through ESP but from the way he knocked.

'You let him in while I find the phone. It's far too early to be ready for court, but maybe he wants to take you out to breakfast.'

She took refuge in her bedroom. Rory at work she could handle. Even Rory seen around the building she could manage. But Rory in her flat when last time he'd been here had been to make love to her?

No, thanks.

Not yet.

Maybe never…

'He wants to see you, and if you're finished in the bathroom I'm going to have a shower and get dressed then we're going to breakfast. Cool, huh?'

Jason imparted this information through the partly open door, and when Alana assured him the bathroom was all his, he disappeared.

Aware she couldn't hide from Rory for ever, Alana left her sanctuary, carrying the phone.

'It's for Jase. So he can ring me.' The words stumbled from her lips as she busied herself programming in her hospital number, then, unable to resist, she looked up into blue eyes that were studying her intently.

'Good luck today,' she said quietly.

'Thank you,' he said, equally grave.

Then he reached out and took the phone from her, set it on the coffee-table and took both her hands in his.

'For everything, Alana,' he murmured, breaking her heart into even smaller pieces.

Determined not to cry, she gritted her teeth, stabbing her tongue into their barrier, concentrating on that rather than the warmth of the fingers holding hers.

'I've got to go,' she managed, when she'd retrieved her hands and her breathing stabilised. 'Tell Jason the number's preset on two.'

She walked back to the bedroom, grabbed her bag, knocked on the bathroom door for a final 'Good luck' to Jason, then, avoiding Rory's eyes this time, she whisked past him and out the door.

*   *   *

The phone call, when it came, was from Kirsten, not Jason.

'Just be prepared. They're on their way to see you. Rory and Jason. Do you look OK? Are there Betadine stains on your uniform? Do you have a clean top in your locker?'

'Kirsten, what are you babbling on about?' Alana demanded, but there was no stopping Kirsten in full flow. Now she was talking about make-up. Was Alana wearing lipstick? No, maybe not, but check her nose. Shiny noses tended to be offputting. And hair—was it up? Of course it was, she was at work. How about she soften it a bit around her face?

'Kirsten, you're obviously either inebriated or you've flipped,' Alana said crossly as the gabble of words became more and more confusing. 'I'm hanging up now.'

And she did.

'What was that about?' Will, the only nurse at the nurses' station at the time, asked.

'I have no idea,' Alana said, then, hearing footsteps, she looked up to see a beaming Jason heading into the ward, with Rory, looking distinctly uncomfortable, trailing along behind.

'You're smiling. You've won?' Alana said to Jason, who nodded, then shook his head while his ears turned pink.

'I think we have,' he said, shifting from foot to foot as if whatever exciting thing had propelled him into the ward had now lost its lustre. 'It's kind of up to you. Rory's cross, but the judge started rabbiting on about him being single and my father's lawyers made it sound like a crime, and Drusilla and Rosemary were there, just waiting for Rory to say he'd marry one of them, and suddenly I knew the answer.'

He gave her a big smile that was only partly apprehensive, while the ear colour deepened towards red.

'I told the judge—it's not like TV courts where the judge sits up high, this was a woman judge and she sat at a table with us. Anyway, I told her Rory was going to get married, and that he hadn't said anything to anyone because he thought it would be best to get the custody settled first. And the judge asked who he was marrying, and I said you.'

The final words came out in such a rush that Alana wasn't sure she'd heard right.

'You said me? You told the judge Rory was going to marry *me*?'

'It needn't be for ever,' Jason said nervously. 'But you do like him, don't you? And he likes you and I like you because you don't fuss over me, so if he's got to marry someone it might as well be you.'

He looked anxiously at Alana and added, 'That's unless just thinking about it makes you want to puke.'

Alana closed her eyes, but when she opened them again, she was still standing in the nurses' station in Eight B, and most of the staff were also standing there, drawn by the drama being played out in front of them. Heaven sent, most of them would think, to enliven their working day.

'Well, does the idea make you want to puke?' Will prompted, and Alana stole a look at Rory.

He remained impassively silent, his face so wiped of all emotion he might have been wearing a mask.

'Not puke exactly,' she ventured, and thought she saw a tiny movement of his lips that just might have been a quickly mastered smile. 'But how does your uncle feel about this idea, Jason? Doesn't he have some say in it?'

Jason, perhaps sensing victory, beamed at her.

'Oh, he says he doesn't mind. He said if he has to marry someone to keep me, he'd rather you than Drusilla or Rosemary. Boy, are those two spitting nails. You should have heard them. I bet by the time we get home they've both packed up and gone.'

'That might save A and E a couple of murder victims,' Rory murmured, while Alana turned and waved her hands to shift the audience on.

'Show's over, gang,' she said, but no one moved, and Mrs Cross, who'd been on her way to see her husband when the fun had begun, said, 'No, it isn't. You haven't answered the boy. You can't expect us to witness the proposal without letting us know your answer.'

'My answer?' Alana said—it was more of a squeak actually. Her voice wasn't working too well. 'And who do you suggest I answer? The proposer, or the poor man who'll be stuck with me if I say yes?'

'I could manage to live with it,' Rory said, and this time he smiled, his eyes dancing with so much delight it was all Alana could do not to shout with the joy of it all.

'So it's a yes?' Mrs Cross persisted, and Alana, not wanting to leave Jason out, turned to him and said, 'It's a great idea, Jase, but right now I've got a lot of work to do before I finish my shift. Let's talk about it later—at home.'

He flashed a smile at her, his ears returning to their normal colour, then, as he accompanied his uncle out of the ward, he swung back to her.

'We could keep both flats then I could use yours as my bachelor pad, and Marcus could come over for jam sessions.'

'We'll talk about it later,' Alana said firmly, while behind Jason's back Rory's face was a mask of horror as he mouthed 'bachelor pad?' at her.

'Later,' Alana repeated, but this time, when she turned back to the desk, prepared to hustle the staff back to work, a burst of clapping broke out and she stood there, flushed with embarrassment, as people, both friends and visitors she barely knew, all wished her well.

The interruption meant it was close to five before Alana left the ward, but as she walked out the staff exit a tall, dark-haired figure with a straight, strong profile peeled himself off the wall and strode to meet her.

'I was beginning to think you'd sneaked out another

door,' Rory said, taking her hand and leading her not towards the footpath but back into the hospital gardens.

Heart a-thump with unexpected excitement, Alana followed, eventually gathering enough breath to ask, 'Where are we going?'

'Just over here,' he told her, acting so in control and manly her knees went weak.

Again!

'I need to talk to you, and if we go home we'll either have Jason organising our lives, or Gabi and Kirsten making wedding plans, or Daisy fretting over the psychological implications of all of this, plus Drusilla and Rosemary having hysterics as they pack.'

They'd reached a garden seat, set so far back beneath the hanging boughs of a yellow jasmine Alana had never noticed it.

'Sit!' he ordered, and though the order was abrupt, Alana read uncertainty in it.

'Will I have to "stay" as well?' she teased, turning to look into his eyes. He sighed, took her in his arms and drew her hard against his chest.

'I hope to hell you will,' he murmured, his lips nuzzling her ear. 'But given all that's been going on, I wouldn't blame you if you wanted to put a couple of oceans and a continent or two between yourself and the Forrester-McAllister duo. The Forrester part particularly.'

'The only thing you've been guilty of was wanting the best for Jason,' Alana reminded him, shifting her head so the nuzzling lips met her own questing ones.

The kiss, a proper one this time, sent heat sizzling through her body, while Rory's fingers, threading into her hair so pins popped out and it tumbled to her shoulders, held her captive in a prison she might never want to leave.

Eventually they broke apart and Alana was grateful for the garden seat because her knees had become very unreliable again. Especially as Rory, far from looking happy, or even satisfied, post-kiss, was eyeing her with a gravity that added butterflies to the mish-mash of stuff going on inside her body.

'Jason's pushed you into this,' he began, then hesitated, looking out across the grounds to where the lights were coming on in the car park. 'He's made it very hard for you to say no. But you can. We'd work out something else. Or we could get married to satisfy the court then annul it if you wanted—'

'Hey!' Alana shifted so she could look into his face, and pressed a finger against his lips to hush him up.

She smiled, though her insides were so nervously over-wrought by now it was an effort.

'I think annulment only works if we don't have sex, and if there's one great advantage to us being married—this is after Saturday night and due consideration of all aspects of it—it would have to be that we can legally go to bed to-gether and enjoy whatever happens there. So annulment's out.'

She paused for breath, looking hopefully into his face, but his mask-look was back.

She tried again.

'So, if we get married, I'd say it has to be for keeps, which suits me because, although I may not have men-tioned it, I love you, Rory Forrester. At first I thought it was just lust—you know, an overwhelming physical attrac-tion—but then I saw you being you, caring for Jason, being kind to Drusilla and Rosemary when any normal man would have tossed them out, even putting up with Kirsten and Gabi interfering in your life.'

She shrugged to lighten the mood and added, 'Actually, now I think about all those things, I have to wonder if you're normal.'

This time she used a kiss as punctuation, before adding, 'But, normal or not, I still love you. There—that's said. Now it's your turn.'

Rory looked so horrified she laughed.

'It can't be that bad. You managed to say some very nice things on Saturday night. And I don't need protestations of undying love, just an acknowledgement that you might feel something for me—that'd be a start.'

Rory wrapped his arm around her and drew her close to his body.

'Something for you?' he said huskily. 'I guess you could say that. In fact, I feel so much love for you I'm terrified marriage might mean I'll lose you. It's not just me you'd be marrying, Alana, but Jason as well—a young man at the very start of his teenage years. Think about it very carefully, because I can't promise you there won't be problems or that we'll always agree about what's best for him. And he definitely won't always agree about what's best for him, and that'll cause more problems.'

'Trying to scare me off?' Alana whispered, nestling against his warm, solid body. She turned to smile at him. 'It's not working. Remember what you said earlier—about Jason pushing me into it? Well, he didn't. All he did was free us from the terrible bind we found ourselves in. He made his choice and left us free to love each other. I know it won't always be easy, but that only makes the challenge greater, and the prize so much more valuable.'

'The prize!' Rory murmured, dropping kisses on her hair. 'And what would that be, my darling?'

'Love!' Alana told him. 'Like this.'

And she turned and claimed his lips and told him things for which there were no words.

LIVE THE EMOTION

Modern Romance™ **Tender Romance**™
...seduction and ...love affairs that
passion guaranteed last a lifetime

Medical Romance™ **Historical Romance**™
...medical drama ...rich, vivid and
on the pulse passionate

Sensual Romance™ *Blaze Romance*™
...sassy, sexy and ...the temperature's
seductive rising

27 new titles every month.

Live the emotion

MILLS & BOON®

MB3

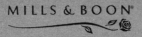

MILLS & BOON®

Medical Romance™

DAISY AND THE DOCTOR *by Meredith Webber*

Dr Julian Austin doesn't believe in love – so psychologist Daisy is his perfect bride. She's been hurt too often to trust in love. Then Daisy realises that, for her, marriage to Julian would be exactly the love match she wants to avoid – and Julian starts to wonder – if love doesn't exist, what's happening to his heart?

THE SURGEON'S MARRIAGE *by Maggie Kingsley*

Doctors Tom and Helen Brooke have a great marriage – when they can find time to see each other. Despite being overworked and under-appreciated, Helen knows she and Tom have something special. Then a series of misunderstandings makes her think that Tom doesn't care – and Tom is faced with a fight to save his marriage…

THE MIDWIFE'S BABY WISH *by Gill Sanderson*

As Keldale's midwife, Lyn Pierce is kept busy! But when Dr Adam Fletcher joins the practice he awakens emotions she can't afford to let herself feel. For it soon becomes clear that Adam wants a family – and while Lyn can give him love, giving him the children he longs for is an impossible dream…

On sale 4th April 2003

Available at most branches of WH Smith, Tesco, Martins, Borders, Eason, Sainsbury's and all good paperback bookshops.

0303/03a

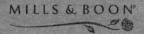

MILLS & BOON

Medical Romance™

DR DALLORI'S BRIDE by *Carol Wood*

For the last six months Dr Antonio Dallori has tried to forget Laura Bright. He met her only once, and was intrigued by their encounter. So he's elated when Laura returns to the village as his new practice nurse! Laura is incredibly attracted to Antonio – but she has a baby to think of now...

DELIVERING SECRETS by *Fiona McArthur*

Midwife Ellie Diamond convinces herself that it is the chance to bring up her son in an idyllic coastal town that has lured her back to Bell's River. It has nothing to do with the chance to work with her former love, obstetrician Dr Luke Farrell – the man Ellie promised to return to five years ago...

HIS EMERGENCY FIANCÉE by *Kate Hardy*

Playboy A&E doctor Ben Robertson needs a fiancée – *quick!* He invented one to keep a certain person happy – and now she is demanding to meet his bride-to-be! Ben has no choice but to beg his housemate, surgeon Kirsty Brown, to play the part. Kirsty agrees – reluctantly. So why is she suddenly wishing she was his real fiancée after all?

On sale 4th April 2003

Available at most branches of WH Smith, Tesco, Martins, Borders, Eason, Sainsbury's and all good paperback bookshops.

0303/03b

MILLS & BOON

dark angel
LYNNE GRAHAM

Knight in shining armour
or avenging angel?

Available from 21st March 2003

*Available at most branches of WH Smith,
Tesco, Martins, Borders, Eason, Sainsbury's
and all good paperback bookshops.*

0403/135/MB68

Become a Panel Member

If YOU are a regular United Kingdom buyer of Mills & Boon®
Medical Romance™ you might like to tell us your opinion of the
books we publish to help us in publishing the books *you* like.

Mills & Boon have a Reader Panel of Medical Romance™ readers.
Each person on the panel receives a short questionnaire (taking
about five minutes to complete) every third month asking for
opinions of the past month's Medical Romances. All people who
send in their replies have a chance of winning a FREE year's supply
of Medical Romances.

If YOU would like to be considered for inclusion on the panel please
fill in and return the following survey. We can't guarantee that
everyone will be on the panel but first come will be first considered.

Where did you buy this novel?

❏ WH Smith
❏ Tesco
❏ Borders
❏ Sainsbury's
❏ Direct by mail
❏ Other (please state) _____

What themes do you enjoy most in the Mills & Boon® novels that
you read? (Choose all that apply.)

❏ Amnesia
❏ Family drama (including babies/young children)
❏ Hidden/Mistaken identity
❏ Historical setting
❏ Marriage of convenience
❏ Medical drama
❏ Mediterranean men
❏ Millionaire heroes
❏ Mock engagement or marriage
❏ Outback setting
❏ Revenge

- ❏ Sheikh heroes
- ❏ Secret baby
- ❏ Shared pasts
- ❏ Western

On average, how many Mills & Boon® novels do you read every month? ————————————————

Please provide us with your name and address:

Name: _____
Address: _____
_____
_____
_____

What is your occupation?
(OPTIONAL)
_____

In which of the following age groups do you belong?
(OPTIONAL)

- ❏ 18 to 24
- ❏ 25 to 34
- ❏ 35 to 49
- ❏ 50 to 64
- ❏ 65 or older

Thank you for your help!
Your feedback is important in helping us offer
quality products you value.

The Reader Service
Reader Panel Questionnaire
FREEPOST CN81
Croydon CR9 3WZ

FREE

2 BOOKS
AND A SURPRISE GIFT!

We would like to take this opportunity to thank you for reading this Mills & Boon® book by offering you the chance to take TWO more specially selected titles from the Medical Romance™ series absolutely FREE! We're also making this offer to introduce you to the benefits of the Reader Service™—

- ★ FREE home delivery
- ★ FREE monthly Newsletter
- ★ FREE gifts and competitions
- ★ Exclusive Reader Service discount
- ★ Books available before they're in the shops

Accepting these FREE books and gift places you under no obligation to buy; you may cancel at any time, even after receiving your free shipment. Simply complete your details below and return the entire page to the address below. *You don't even need a stamp!*

YES! Please send me 2 free Medical Romance books and a surprise gift. I understand that unless you hear from me, I will receive 4 superb new titles every month for just £2.60 each, postage and packing free. I am under no obligation to purchase any books and may cancel my subscription at any time. The free books and gift will be mine to keep in any case.

M3ZEC

Ms/Mrs/Miss/Mr ....Initials ....
BLOCK CAPITALS PLEASE

Surname ....

Address ....

....

....Postcode ....

Send this whole page to:
UK: FREEPOST CN81, Croydon, CR9 3WZ
EIRE: PO Box 4546, Kilcock, County Kildare (stamp required)

Offer valid in UK and Eire only and not available to current Reader Service subscribers to this series. We reserve the right to refuse an application and applicants must be aged 18 years or over. Only one application per household. Terms and prices subject to change without notice. Offer expires 30th June 2003. As a result of this application, you may receive offers from Harlequin Mills & Boon and other carefully selected companies. If you would prefer not to share in this opportunity please write to The Data Manager at the address above.

Mills & Boon® is a registered trademark owned by Harlequin Mills & Boon Limited.
Medical Romance™ is being used as a trademark.